Supernatural
Short Stories

Supernatural Short Stories

Charles Dickens

ALMA CLASSICS

ALMA CLASSICS LTD
London House
243-253 Lower Mortlake Road
Richmond
Surrey TW9 2LL
United Kingdom
www.almaclassics.com

This edition first published by Alma Classics Ltd in 2012

Cover image © Getty Images

Extra material © Alma Classics Ltd

Printed and bound by CPI Group (UK) Ltd, Croydon, CR0 4YY

Typeset by Tetragon

ISBN: 978-1-84749-227-2

Contents

The Bagman's Story   3

The Story of the Goblins Who Stole a Sexton   19

The Story of the Bagman's Uncle   31

The Baron of Grogzwig   49

A Confession Found in a Prison in the Time   59
of Charles II

To Be Read at Dusk   67

The Ghost in the Bride's Chamber   79

The Haunted House   97

To Be Taken with a Grain of Salt   129

No. 1. Branch Line: The Signalman   141

Note on the Texts   155

Notes   155

Extra Material   157

   Charles Dickens's Life   159

   Charles Dickens's Works   167

   Select Bibliography   173

Charles Dickens (1812–70)

John Dickens,
Charles's father

Elizabeth Dickens,
Charles's mother

Catherine Dickens,
Charles's wife

Ellen Ternan

1 Mile End Terrace, Portsmouth, Dickens's birthplace (above left),
48 Doughty Street, London, Dickens's home 1837–39 (above right)
and Tavistock House, London, Dickens's residence 1851–60 (below)

Gad's Hill Place, Kent, where Dickens lived from 1857 to 1870 (above)
and the author in his study at Gad's Hill Place (below)

Supernatural
Short Stories

The Bagman's Story*

O NE WINTER'S EVENING, about five o'clock, just as it began
to grow dusk, a man in a gig might have been seen urging his
tired horse along the road which leads across Marlborough Downs,
in the direction of Bristol. I say he might have been seen, and I
have no doubt he would have been, if anybody but a blind man
had happened to pass that way; but the weather was so bad, and
the night so cold and wet, that nothing was out but the water, and
so the traveller jogged along in the middle of the road, lonesome
and dreary enough. If any bagman of that day could have caught
sight of the little neck-or-nothing sort of gig, with a clay-coloured
body and red wheels, and the vixenish ill-tempered, fast-going
bay mare, that looked like a cross between a butcher's horse and
a two-penny post-office pony, he would have known at once that
this traveller could have been no other than Tom Smart, of the
great house of Bilson and Slum, Cateaton Street, City. However,
as there was no bagman to look on, nobody knew anything at all
about the matter; and so Tom Smart and his clay-coloured gig
with the red wheels, and the vixenish mare with the fast pace,
went on together, keeping the secret among them – and nobody
was a bit the wiser.

There are many pleasanter places even in this dreary world than
Marlborough Downs when it blows hard; and if you throw in
beside, a gloomy winter's evening, a miry and sloppy road and a
pelting fall of heavy rain, and try the effect, by way of experiment,
in your own proper person, you will experience the full force of
this observation.

The wind blew – not up the road or down it, though that's bad
enough, but sheer across it, sending the rain slanting down like the
lines they used to rule in the copy books at school, to make the
boys slope well. For a moment it would die away, and the traveller

3

would begin to delude himself into the belief that, exhausted with its previous fury, it had quietly lain itself down to rest, when – whoo! – he would hear it growling and whistling in the distance, and on it would come rushing over the hilltops and sweeping along the plain, gathering sound and strength as it drew nearer, until it dashed with a heavy gust against horse and man, driving the sharp rain into their ears and its cold damp breath into their very bones – and past them it would scour, far, far away, with a stunning roar, as if in ridicule of their weakness, and triumphant in the consciousness of its own strength and power.

The bay mare splashed away, through the mud and water, with drooping ears, now and then tossing her head as if to express her disgust at this very ungentlemanly behaviour of the elements, but keeping a good pace notwithstanding, until a gust of wind, more furious than any that had yet assailed them, caused her to stop suddenly and plant her four feet firmly against the ground, to prevent her being blown over. It's a special mercy that she did this, for if she *had* been blown over, the vixenish mare was so light, and the gig was so light, and Tom Smart such a light weight into the bargain, that they must infallibly have all gone rolling over and over together, until they reached the confines of earth, or until the wind fell – and in either case the probability is that neither the vixenish mare, nor the clay-coloured gig with the red wheels, nor Tom Smart, would ever have been fit for service again.

"Well, damn my straps and whiskers," says Tom Smart (Tom sometimes had an unpleasant knack of swearing). "Damn my straps and whiskers," says Tom, "if this ain't pleasant, blow me!"

You'll very likely ask me why, as Tom Smart had been pretty well blown already, he expressed this wish to be submitted to the same process again. I can't say – all I know is that Tom Smart said so – or at least he always told my uncle he said so, and it's just the same thing.

"Blow me," says Tom Smart, and the mare neighed as if she were precisely of the same opinion.

"Cheer up, old girl," said Tom, patting the bay mare on the neck with the end of his whip. "It won't do pushing on, such a night as this; the first house we come to we'll put up at, so the faster you go the sooner it's over. Soho, old girl – gently – gently."

Whether the vixenish mare was sufficiently well acquainted with the tones of Tom's voice to comprehend his meaning, or whether she found it colder standing still than moving on, of course I can't say. But I can say that Tom had no sooner finished speaking than she pricked up her ears and started forward at a speed which made the clay-coloured gig rattle till you would have supposed every one of the red spokes were going to fly out on the turf of Marlborough Downs; and even Tom, whip as he was, couldn't stop or check her pace, until she drew up, of her own accord, before a roadside inn on the right-hand side of the way, about half a quarter of a mile from the end of the Downs.

Tom cast a hasty glance at the upper part of the house as he threw the reins to the hostler and stuck the whip in the box. It was a strange old place, built of a kind of shingle – inlaid, as it were, with cross-beams, with gabled-topped windows projecting completely over the pathway and a low door with a dark porch, and a couple of steep steps leading down into the house, instead of the modern fashion of a half a dozen ones leading up to it. It was a comfortable-looking place though, for there was a strong cheerful light in the bar window, which shed a bright ray across the road and even lighted up the hedges on the other side; and there was a red flickering light in the opposite window, one moment but faintly discernible, and the next gleaming strongly through the drawn curtains, which intimated that a rousing fire was blazing within. Marking these little evidences with the eye of an experienced traveller, Tom dismounted with as much agility as his half-frozen limbs would permit and entered the house.

In less than five minutes' time, Tom was ensconced in the room opposite the bar – the very room where he had imagined the fire blazing – before a substantial matter-of-fact roaring fire, composed of something short of a bushel of coals, and wood enough to make half a dozen decent gooseberry bushes, piled halfway up the chimney, and roaring and crackling with a sound that of itself would have warmed the heart of any reasonable man. This was comfortable, but this was not all, for a smartly dressed girl, with a bright eye and a neat ankle, was laying a very clean white cloth on the table; and as Tom sat with his slippered feet on the fender and his back to the open door, he saw a charming prospect of the bar reflected in the glass over the chimney piece, with delightful rows of green bottles and gold labels, together with jars of pickles and preserves, and cheeses and boiled hams, and rounds of beef, arranged on shelves in the most tempting and delicious array. Well, this was comfortable too, but even this was not all – for in the bar, seated at tea at the nicest possible little table, drawn close up before the brightest possible little fire, was a buxom widow of somewhere about eight-and-forty or thereabouts, with a face as comfortable as the bar, who was evidently the landlady of the house and the supreme ruler over all these agreeable possessions. There was only one drawback to the beauty of the whole picture, and that was a tall man – a very tall man – in a brown coat and bright basket buttons, and black whiskers, and wavy black hair, who was seated at tea with the widow, and who it required no great penetration to discover was in a fair way of persuading her to be a widow no longer, but to confer upon him the privilege of sitting down in that bar for and during the whole remainder of the term of his natural life.

Tom Smart was by no means of an irritable or envious disposition, but somehow or other the tall man with the brown coat and the bright basket buttons did rouse what little gall he had in his composition, and did make him feel extremely indignant: the more especially as he could now and then observe, from his seat before the glass, certain little affectionate familiarities passing between the tall man and the widow, which sufficiently denoted that the tall man was as high in favour as he was in size. Tom was fond of hot punch – I may venture to say he was *very* fond of hot punch – and after he had seen the vixenish mare well fed and well littered down, and had eaten every bit of the nice little hot dinner which the widow tossed up for him with her own hands, he just ordered a tumbler of it, by way of experiment. Now, if there was one thing in the whole range of domestic art which the widow could manufacture better than another, it was this identical article; and the first tumbler was adapted to Tom Smart's taste with such peculiar nicety that he ordered a second with the least possible delay. Hot punch is a pleasant thing, gentlemen – an extremely pleasant thing under any circumstances – but in that snug old parlour, before the roaring fire, with the wind blowing outside till every timber in the old house creaked again, Tom Smart found it perfectly delightful. He ordered another tumbler, and then another – I am not quite certain whether he didn't order another after that – but the more he drank of the hot punch, the more he thought of the tall man.

"Confound his impudence!" said Tom to himself. "What business has he in that snug bar? Such an ugly villain too!" said Tom. "If the widow had any taste, she might surely pick up some better fellow than that." Here Tom's eye wandered from the glass on the chimney piece to the glass on the table; and as he felt himself becoming gradually sentimental, he emptied the fourth tumbler of punch and ordered a fifth.

Tom Smart, gentlemen, had always been very much attached to the public line. It had long been his ambition to stand in a bar of his own, in a green coat, knee-cords and tops. He had a great notion of taking the chair at convivial dinners, and he had often thought how well he could preside in a room of his own in the talking way, and what a capital example he could set to his customers in the drinking department. All these things passed rapidly through Tom's mind as he sat drinking the hot punch by the roaring fire, and he felt very justly and properly indignant that the tall man should be in a fair way of keeping such an excellent house, while he, Tom Smart, was as far off from it as ever. So, after deliberating over the two last tumblers, whether he hadn't a perfect right to pick a quarrel with the tall man for having contrived to get into the good graces of the buxom widow, Tom Smart at last arrived at the satisfactory conclusion that he was a very ill-used and persecuted individual, and had better go to bed.

Up a wide and ancient staircase the smart girl preceded Tom, shading the chamber candle with her hand, to protect it from the currents of air which in such a rambling old place might have found plenty of room to disport themselves in, without blowing the candle out – but which did blow it out nevertheless, thus affording Tom's enemies an opportunity of asserting that it was he, and not the wind, who extinguished the candle, and that while he pretended to be blowing it alight again, he was in fact kissing the girl. Be this as it may, another light was obtained, and Tom was conducted through a maze of rooms and a labyrinth of passages to the apartment which had been prepared for his reception, where the girl bade him good night and left him alone.

It was a good large room with big closets, and a bed which might have served for a whole boarding school, to say nothing of a couple of oaken presses that would have held the baggage of a small army; but what struck Tom's fancy most was a strange, grim-looking high-backed chair, carved in the most fantastic manner, with a flowered damask cushion and the round knobs at the bottom of the legs carefully tied up in red cloth, as if it had got the gout in its toes. Of any other queer chair, Tom would only have thought it *was* a queer chair, and there would have been an end of the matter; but there was something about this particular chair, and yet he couldn't tell what it was, so odd and so unlike any other piece of furniture he had ever seen, that it seemed to fascinate him. He sat down before the fire and stared at the old chair for half an hour – Deuce take the chair: it was such a strange old thing, he couldn't take his eyes off it.

"Well," said Tom, slowly undressing himself and staring at the old chair all the while, which stood with a mysterious aspect by the bedside, "I never saw such a rum concern as that in my days. Very odd," said Tom, who had got rather sage with the hot punch. "Very odd." Tom shook his head with an air of profound wisdom and looked at the chair again. He couldn't make anything of it though, so he got into bed, covered himself up warm and fell asleep.

In about half an hour, Tom woke up with a start from a confused dream of tall men and tumblers of punch: and the first object that presented itself to his waking imagination was the queer chair.

"I won't look at it any more," said Tom to himself, and he squeezed his eyelids together and tried to persuade himself he was going to sleep again. No use: nothing but queer chairs danced before his eyes, kicking up their legs, jumping over each other's backs and playing all kinds of antics.

"I may as well see one real chair as two or three complete sets of false ones," said Tom, bringing out his head from under the bedclothes. There it was, plainly discernible by the light of the fire, looking as provoking as ever.

Tom gazed at the chair, and suddenly, as he looked at it, a most extraordinary change seemed to come over it. The carving of the back gradually assumed the lineaments and expression of an old shrivelled human face; the damask cushion became an antique, flapped waistcoat; the round knobs grew into a couple of feet, encased in red-cloth slippers; and the old chair looked like a very ugly old man of the previous century, with his arms akimbo. Tom sat up in bed and rubbed his eyes to dispel the illusion. No. The chair was an ugly old gentleman – and what was more, he was winking at Tom Smart.

Tom was naturally a headlong, careless sort of dog, and he had had five tumblers of hot punch into the bargain; so, although he was a little startled at first, he began to grow rather indignant when he saw the old gentleman winking and leering at him with such an impudent air. At length he resolved that he wouldn't stand it; and as the old face still kept winking away as fast as ever, Tom said, in a very angry tone:

"What the devil are you winking at me for?"

"Because I like it, Tom Smart," said the chair – or the old gentleman, whichever you like to call him. He stopped winking though, when Tom spoke, and began grinning like a superannuated monkey.

"How do you know my name, old nut-cracker face!" enquired Tom Smart, rather staggered – though he pretended to carry it off so well.

"Come, come, Tom," said the old gentleman, "that's not the way to address solid Spanish mahogany. Dam' me, you couldn't treat me with less respect if I was veneered." When the old gentleman said this, he looked so fierce that Tom began to grow frightened.

"I didn't mean to treat you with any disrespect, sir," said Tom, in a much humbler tone than he had spoken in at first.

"Well, well," said the old fellow, "perhaps not – perhaps not. Tom…"

"Sir…"

"I know everything about you, Tom – everything. You're very poor, Tom."

"I certainly am," said Tom Smart. "But how came you to know that?"

"Never mind that," said the old gentleman. "You're much too fond of punch, Tom."

Tom Smart was just on the point of protesting that he hadn't tasted a drop since his last birthday, but when his eye encountered that of the old gentleman, he looked so knowing that Tom blushed and was silent.

"Tom," said the old gentleman, "the widow's a fine woman – remarkably fine woman – eh, Tom?" Here the old fellow screwed up his eyes, cocked up one of his wasted little legs, and looked altogether so unpleasantly amorous that Tom was quite disgusted with the levity of his behaviour – at his time of life, too!

"I am her guardian, Tom," said the old gentleman.

"Are you?" enquired Tom Smart.

"I knew her mother, Tom," said the old fellow, "and her grand-mother. She was very fond of me – made me this waistcoat, Tom."

"Did she?" said Tom Smart.

"And these shoes," said the old fellow, lifting up one of the red-cloth mufflers. "But don't mention it, Tom. I shouldn't like to have it known that she was so much attached to me. It might occasion some unpleasantness in the family." When the old rascal said this, he looked so extremely impertinent that, as Tom Smart afterwards declared, he could have sat upon him without remorse.

"I have been a great favourite among the women in my time, Tom," said the profligate old debauchee. "Hundreds of fine women have sat in my lap for hours together. What do you think of that, you dog, eh!" The old gentleman was proceeding to recount some other exploits of his youth, when he was seized with such a violent fit of creaking that he was unable to proceed.

"Just served you right, old boy," thought Tom Smart – but he didn't say anything.

"Ah!" said the old fellow, "I am a good deal troubled with this now. I am getting old, Tom, and have lost nearly all my rails. I have had an operation performed, too – a small piece let into my back – and I found it a severe trial, Tom."

"I dare say you did, sir," said Tom Smart.

"However," said the old gentleman, "that's not the point. Tom! I want you to marry the widow."

"Me, sir!" said Tom.

"You," said the old gentleman.

"Bless your reverend locks," said Tom – (he had a few scattered horse hairs left) – "bless your reverend locks, she wouldn't have me." And Tom sighed involuntarily, as he thought of the bar.

"Wouldn't she?" said the old gentleman, firmly.

"No, no," said Tom. "There's somebody else in the wind. A tall man – a confoundedly tall man – with black whiskers."

"Tom," said the old gentleman, "she will never have him."

"Won't she?" said Tom. "If you stood in the bar, old gentleman, you'd tell another story."

"Pooh, pooh," said the old gentleman. "I know all about that."

"About what?" said Tom.

"About kissing behind the door, and all that sort of thing, Tom," said the old gentleman. And here he gave another impudent look, which made Tom very wroth, because as you all know, gentlemen, to hear an old fellow, who ought to know better, talking about these things is very unpleasant – nothing more so.

"I know all about that, Tom," said the old gentleman. "I have seen it done very often in my time, Tom, between more people than I should like to mention to you – but it never came to anything after all."

"You must have seen some queer things," said Tom, with an inquisitive look.

"You may say that, Tom," replied the old fellow, with a very complicated wink. "I am the last of my family, Tom," said the old gentleman, with a melancholy sigh.

"Was it a large one?" enquired Tom Smart.

"There were twelve of us, Tom," said the old gentleman, "fine straight-backed, handsome fellows as you'd wish to see. None of your modern abortions – all with arms, and with a degree of polish (though I say it that should not) which would have done your heart good to behold."

"And what's become of the others, sir?" asked Tom Smart.

The old gentleman applied his elbow to his eye as he replied: "Gone, Tom, gone. We had hard service, Tom, and they hadn't all my constitution. They got rheumatic about the legs and arms, and went into kitchens and hospitals; and one of 'em, with long service and hard usage, positively lost his senses – he got so crazy that he was obliged to be burnt. Shocking thing that, Tom."

"Dreadful!" said Tom Smart.

The old fellow paused for a few minutes, apparently struggling with his feelings of emotion, and then said:

"However, Tom, I am wandering from the point. This tall man, Tom, is a rascally adventurer. The moment he married the widow, he would sell off all the furniture and run away. What would be the consequence? She would be deserted and reduced to ruin, and I should catch my death of cold in some broker's shop."

"Yes, but…"

"Don't interrupt me," said the old gentleman. "Of you, Tom, I entertain a very different opinion, for I well know that if you once settled yourself in a public house, you would never leave it, as long as there was anything to drink within its walls."

"I am very much obliged to you for your good opinion, sir," said Tom Smart.

"Therefore," resumed the old gentleman, in a dictatorial tone, "you shall have her, and he shall not."

"What is to prevent it?" said Tom Smart, eagerly.

"This disclosure," replied the old gentleman. "He is already married."

"How can I prove it?" said Tom, starting half out of bed.

The old gentleman untucked his arm from his side and, having pointed to one of the oaken presses, immediately replaced it in its old position.

"He little thinks," said the old gentleman, "that in the right-hand pocket of a pair of trousers in that press he has left a letter, entreating him to return to his disconsolate wife, with six – mark me, Tom – six babes, and all of them small ones."

As the old gentleman solemnly uttered these words, his features grew less and less distinct, and his figure more shadowy. A film came over Tom Smart's eyes. The old man seemed gradually blending into the chair, the damask waistcoat to resolve into a cushion, the red slippers to shrink into little red-cloth bags. The light faded gently away, and Tom Smart fell back on his pillow and dropped asleep.

Morning aroused Tom from the lethargic slumber into which he had fallen on the disappearance of the old man. He sat up in bed, and for some minutes vainly endeavoured to recall the events of the preceding night. Suddenly they rushed upon him. He looked at the chair: it was a fantastic and grim-looking piece of furniture, certainly, but it must have been a remarkably ingenious and lively imagination that could have discovered any resemblance between it and an old man.

"How are you, old boy?" said Tom. He was bolder in the daylight – most men are.

The chair remained motionless, and spoke not a word.

"Miserable morning," said Tom. No. The chair would not be drawn into conversation.

"Which press did you point to? You can tell me that," said Tom. Devil a word, gentlemen, the chair would say.

"It's not much trouble to open it, anyhow," said Tom, getting out of bed very deliberately. He walked up to one of the presses. The key was in the lock; he turned it and opened the door. There *was* a pair of trousers there. He put his hand into the pocket, and drew forth the identical letter the old gentleman had described!

"Queer sort of thing, this," said Tom Smart, looking first at the chair and then at the press, and then at the letter, and then at the chair again. "Very queer," said Tom. But, as there was nothing in either to lessen the queerness, he thought he might as well dress himself and settle the tall man's business at once – just to put him out of his misery.

Tom surveyed the rooms he passed through, on his way downstairs, with the scrutinizing eye of a landlord, thinking it not impossible that before long they and their contents would be his property. The tall man was standing in the snug little bar with his hands behind him, quite at home. He grinned vacantly at Tom. A casual observer might have supposed he did it only to show his white teeth, but Tom Smart thought that a consciousness of triumph was passing through the place where the tall man's mind would have been, if he had had any. Tom laughed in his face, and summoned the landlady.

"Good morning, ma'am," said Tom Smart, closing the door of the little parlour as the widow entered.

"Good morning, sir," said the widow. "What will you take for breakfast, sir?"

Tom was thinking how he should open the case, so he made no answer.

"There's a very nice ham," said the widow, "and a beautiful cold larded fowl. Shall I send 'em in, sir?"

These words roused Tom from his reflections. His admiration of the widow increased as she spoke. Thoughtful creature! Comfortable provider!

"Who is that gentleman in the bar, ma'am?" enquired Tom.

"His name is Jinkins, sir," said the widow, slightly blushing.

"He's a tall man," said Tom.

"He is a very fine man, sir," replied the widow, "and a very nice gentleman."

"Ah!" said Tom.

"Is there anything more you want, sir?" enquired the widow, rather puzzled by Tom's manner.

"Why, yes," said Tom. "My dear ma'am, will you have the kindness to sit down for one moment?"

The widow looked much amazed, but she sat down, and Tom sat down too, close beside her. I don't know how it happened, gentlemen – indeed my uncle used to tell me that Tom Smart said *he* didn't know how it happened either – but somehow or other the palm of Tom's hand fell upon the back of the widow's hand and remained there while he spoke.

"My dear ma'am," said Tom Smart – he had always a great notion of committing the amiable. "My dear ma'am, you deserve a very excellent husband – you do indeed."

"Lor, sir!" said the widow – as well she might: Tom's mode of commencing the conversation being rather unusual, not to say startling, the fact of his never having set eyes upon her before the previous night being taken into consideration. "Lor, sir!"

"I scorn to flatter, my dear ma'am," said Tom Smart. "You deserve a very admirable husband, and whoever he is, he'll be a very lucky man." As Tom said this, his eye involuntarily wandered from the widow's face to the comforts around him.

The widow looked more puzzled than ever, and made an effort to rise. Tom gently pressed her hand, as if to detain her, and she kept her seat. Widows, gentlemen, are not usually timorous, as my uncle used to say.

"I am sure I am very much obliged to you, sir, for your good opinion," said the buxom landlady, half laughing, "and if ever I marry again…"

"*If*," said Tom Smart, looking very shrewdly out of the right-hand corner of his left eye. "*If*…"

"Well," said the widow, laughing outright this time. "*When* I do, I hope I shall have as good a husband as you describe."

"Jinkins to wit," said Tom.

"Lor, sir!" exclaimed the widow.

"Oh, don't tell me," said Tom, "I know him."

"I am sure nobody who knows him knows anything bad of him," said the widow, bridling up at the mysterious air with which Tom had spoken.

"Hem!" said Tom Smart.

The widow began to think it was high time to cry, so she took out her handkerchief and enquired whether Tom wished to insult her – whether he thought it like a gentleman to take away the character of another gentleman behind his back – why, if he had got anything to say, he didn't say it to the man, like a man, instead of terrifying a poor weak woman in that way – and so forth.

"I'll say it to him fast enough," said Tom, "only I want you to hear it first."

"What is it?" enquired the widow, looking intently in Tom's countenance.

"I'll astonish you," said Tom, putting his hand in his pocket.

"If it is that he wants money," said the widow, "I know that already, and you needn't trouble yourself."

"Pooh, nonsense, that's nothing," said Tom Smart. "*I* want money. 'T an't that."

"Oh, dear, what can it be?" exclaimed the poor widow.

"Don't be frightened," said Tom Smart. He slowly drew forth the letter and unfolded it. "You won't scream?" said Tom, doubtfully.

"No, no," replied the widow, "let me see it."

"You won't go fainting away, or any of that nonsense?" said Tom.

"No, no," returned the widow, hastily.

"And don't run out and blow him up," said Tom, "because I'll do all that for you – you had better not exert yourself."

"Well, well," said the widow, "let me see it."

"I will," replied Tom Smart – and, with these words, he placed the letter in the widow's hand.

Gentlemen, I have heard my uncle say that Tom Smart said the widow's lamentations when she heard the disclosure would have pierced a heart of stone. Tom was certainly very tender-hearted, but they pierced his, to the very core. The widow rocked herself to and fro and wrung her hands.

"Oh, the deception and villainy of man!" said the widow.

"Frightful, my dear ma'am – but compose yourself," said Tom Smart.

"Oh, I can't compose myself," shrieked the widow. "I shall never find anyone else I can love so much!"

"Oh, yes you will, my dear soul," said Tom Smart, letting fall a shower of the largest-sized tears, in pity for the widow's misfortunes. Tom Smart, in the energy of his compassion, had put his arm round the widow's waist – and the widow, in a passion of grief, had clasped Tom's hand. She looked up in Tom's face and smiled through her tears. Tom looked down in hers, and smiled through his.

I could never find out, gentlemen, whether Tom did or did not kiss the widow at that particular moment. He used to tell my uncle he didn't, but I have my doubts about it. Between ourselves, gentlemen, I rather think he did.

At all events, Tom kicked the very tall man out at the front door half an hour after, and married the widow a month after. And he used to drive about the country, with the clay-coloured gig with red wheels, and the vixenish mare with the fast pace, till he gave up business many years afterwards and went to France with his wife – and then the old house was pulled down.

The Story of the Goblins
Who Stole a Sexton*

IN AN OLD ABBEY TOWN, down in this part of the country, a long, long while ago – so long that the story must be a true one, because our great-grandfathers implicitly believed it – there officiated as sexton and grave-digger in the churchyard one Gabriel Grub. It by no means follows that because a man is a sexton, and constantly surrounded by the emblems of mortality, therefore he should be a morose and melancholy man; your undertakers are the merriest fellows in the world – and I once had the honour of being on intimate terms with a mute who in private life, and off duty, was as comical and jocose a little fellow as ever chirped out a devil-may-care song without a hitch in his memory, or drained off the contents of a good stiff glass without stopping for breath. But, notwithstanding these precedents to the contrary, Gabriel Grub was an ill-conditioned, cross-grained, surly fellow – a morose and lonely man who consorted with nobody but himself and an old wicker bottle which fitted into his large waistcoat pocket – and who eyed each merry face, as it passed him by, with such a deep scowl of malice and ill-humour as it was difficult to meet without feeling something the worse for.

A little before twilight, one Christmas Eve, Gabriel shouldered his spade, lighted his lantern and betook himself towards the old churchyard, for he had got a grave to finish by next morning, and feeling very low, he thought it might raise his spirits, perhaps, if he went on with his work at once. As he went his way, up the ancient street, he saw the cheerful light of the blazing fires gleam through the old casements and heard the loud laugh and the cheerful shouts of those who were assembled around them; he marked the bustling preparations for next day's cheer, and smelt the numerous savoury odours consequent thereupon, as they steamed up from the kitchen windows in clouds. All this was gall and wormwood to the heart of Gabriel Grub, and when groups of children bounded out of the houses, tripped across the road and were met, before they could knock at the opposite door, by half a dozen curly-headed little rascals who crowded round them as they flocked upstairs to spend the evening in their Christmas games, Gabriel smiled grimly and clutched the handle of his spade with a firmer grasp, as he thought of measles, scarlet fever, thrush, hooping cough and a good many other sources of consolation besides.

In this happy frame of mind Gabriel strode along, returning a short, sullen growl to the good-humoured greetings of such of his neighbours as now and then passed him, until he turned into the dark lane which led to the churchyard. Now, Gabriel had been looking forward to reaching the dark lane, because it was, generally speaking, a nice, gloomy, mournful place, into which the townspeople did not much care to go except in broad daylight and when the sun was shining; consequently, he was not a little indignant to hear a young urchin roaring out some jolly song about a merry Christmas in this very sanctuary which had been called Coffin Lane ever since the days of the old abbey, and the time of the shaven-headed monks. As Gabriel walked on and the voice grew nearer, he found it proceeded from a small boy who was hurrying alone to join one of the little parties in the old street, and who, partly to keep himself company and partly to prepare himself for the occasion, was shouting out the song at the highest pitch of his lungs. So Gabriel waited until the boy came up, and then dodged him into a corner and rapped him over the head with his lantern five or six times to teach him to modulate his voice. And as the boy hurried away with his hand to his head, singing quite a different sort of tune, Gabriel Grub chuckled very heartily to himself and entered the churchyard, locking the gate behind him.

He took off his coat, put down his lantern and, getting into the unfinished grave, worked at it for an hour or so, with right goodwill. But the earth was hardened with the frost, and it was no very easy matter to break it up and shovel it out; and although there was a moon, it was a very young one, and shed little light upon the grave, which was in the shadow of the church. At any other time, these obstacles would have made Gabriel Grub very moody and miserable, but he was so well pleased with having stopped the small boy's singing that he took little heed of the scanty progress he had made, and looked down into the grave, when he had finished work for the night, with grim satisfaction, murmuring as he gathered up his things:

"Brave lodgings for one, brave lodgings for one,
A few feet of cold earth, when life is done;
A stone at the head, a stone at the feet,
A rich, juicy meal for the worms to eat;
Rank grass overhead and damp clay around,
Brave lodgings for one, these, in holy ground!"

"Ho! ho!" laughed Gabriel Grub, as he sat himself down on a flat tombstone which was a favourite resting place of his, and drew forth his wicker bottle. "A coffin at Christmas! A Christmas Box. Ho! ho! ho!"

"Ho! ho! ho!" repeated a voice which sounded close behind him.

Gabriel paused, in some alarm, in the act of raising the wicker bottle to his lips, and looked round. The bottom of the oldest grave about him was not more still and quiet than the churchyard in the pale moonlight. The cold hoar frost glistened on the tombstones and sparkled like rows of gems among the stone carvings of the old church. The snow lay hard and crisp upon the ground, and spread over the thickly strewn mounds of earth so white and smooth a cover that it seemed as if corpses lay there, hidden only by the winding sheets. Not the faintest rustle broke the profound tranquillity of the solemn scene. Sound itself appeared to be frozen up, all was so cold and still.

"It was the echoes," said Gabriel Grub, raising the bottle to his lips again.

"It was *not*," said a deep voice.

Gabriel started up and stood rooted to the spot with astonishment and terror, for his eyes rested on a form that made his blood run cold.

Seated on an upright tombstone, close to him, was a strange, unearthly figure, whom Gabriel felt at once was no being of this world. His long fantastic legs, which might have reached the ground, were cocked up and crossed after a quaint, fantastic fashion; his sinewy arms were bare, and his hands rested on his knees. On his short round body he wore a close covering, ornamented with small slashes; a short cloak dangled at his back; the collar was cut into curious peaks, which served the goblin in lieu of ruff or neckerchief; and his shoes curled up at his toes into long points. On his head, he wore a broad-brimmed sugar-loaf hat, garnished with a single feather. The hat was covered with the white frost; and the goblin looked as if he had sat on the same tombstone very comfortably for two or three hundred years. He was sitting perfectly still; his tongue was put out, as if in derision, and he was grinning at Gabriel Grub with such a grin as only a goblin could call up.

"It was *not* the echoes," said the goblin.

Gabriel Grub was paralysed and could make no reply.

"What do you do here on Christmas Eve?" said the goblin sternly.

"I come to dig a grave, sir," stammered Gabriel Grub.

"What man wanders among graves and churchyards on such a night as this?" cried the goblin.

"Gabriel Grub! Gabriel Grub!" screamed a wild chorus of voices that seemed to fill the churchyard. Gabriel looked fearfully round – nothing was to be seen.

"What have you got in that bottle?" said the goblin.

"Hollands, sir," replied the sexton, trembling more than ever, for he had bought it of the smugglers, and he thought that perhaps his questioner might be in the excise department of the goblins.

"Who drinks Hollands alone, and in a churchyard, on such a night as this?" said the goblin.

"Gabriel Grub! Gabriel Grub!" exclaimed the wild voices again.

The goblin leered maliciously at the terrified sexton, and then, raising his voice, exclaimed:

"And who, then, is our fair and lawful prize?"

To this enquiry the invisible chorus replied in a strain that sounded like the voices of many choristers singing to the mighty swell of the old church organ – a strain that seemed borne to the sexton's ears upon a wild wind, and to die away as it passed onwards; but the burden of the reply was still the same: "Gabriel Grub! Gabriel Grub!"

The goblin grinned a broader grin than before, as he said: "Well, Gabriel, what do you say to this?"

The sexton gasped for breath.

"What do you think of this, Gabriel?" said the goblin, kicking up his feet in the air on either side of the tombstone and looking at the turned-up points with as much complacency as if he had been contemplating the most fashionable pair of Wellingtons in all Bond Street.

"It's – it's – very curious, sir," replied the sexton, half dead with fright, "very curious, and very pretty, but I think I'll go back and finish my work, sir, if you please."

"Work!" said the goblin. "What work?"

"The grave, sir – making the grave," stammered the sexton.

"Oh, the grave, eh?" said the goblin. "Who makes graves at a time when all other men are merry, and takes a pleasure in it?"

Again the mysterious voices replied, "Gabriel Grub! Gabriel Grub!"

"I'm afraid my friends want you, Gabriel," said the goblin, thrusting his tongue further into his cheek than ever – and a most astonishing tongue it was – "I'm afraid my friends want you, Gabriel," said the goblin.

"Under favour, sir," replied the horror-stricken sexton, "I don't think they can, sir; they don't know me, sir; I don't think the gentlemen have ever seen me, sir."

"Oh, yes they have," replied the goblin. "We know the man with the sulky face and grim scowl that came down the street tonight, throwing his evil looks at the children and grasping his burying spade the tighter. We know the man who struck the boy in the envious malice of his heart, because the boy could be merry and he could not. We know him, we know him."

Here the goblin gave a loud shrill laugh, which the echoes returned twentyfold, and throwing his legs up in the air, stood upon his head, or rather upon the very point of his sugar-loaf hat, on the narrow edge of the tombstone – whence he threw a somerset with extraordinary agility, right to the sexton's feet, at which he planted himself in the attitude in which tailors generally sit upon the shop board.

"I – I – am afraid I must leave you, sir," said the sexton, making an effort to move.

"Leave us!" said the goblin. "Gabriel Grub going to leave us. Ho! ho! ho!"

As the goblin laughed, the sexton observed, for one instant, a brilliant illumination within the windows of the church, as if the whole building were lighted up; it disappeared, the organ pealed forth a lively air, and whole troops of goblins, the very counterpart of the first one, poured into the churchyard and began playing at leap-frog with the tombstones, never stopping for an instant to take breath, but overing the highest among them, one after the other, with the utmost marvellous dexterity. The first goblin was a most astonishing leaper, and none of the others could come near him; even in the extremity of his terror the sexton could not help observing that while his friends were content to leap over the common-sized gravestones, the first one took the family vaults, iron railings and all, with as much ease as if they had been so many street posts.

At last the game reached to a most exciting pitch; the organ played quicker and quicker, and the goblins leapt faster and faster, coiling themselves up, rolling head over heels upon the ground and bounding over the tombstones like footballs. The sexton's brain whirled round with the rapidity of the motion he beheld, and his legs reeled beneath him as the spirits flew before his eyes – when the goblin king, suddenly darting towards him, laid his hand upon his collar and sank with him through the earth.

When Gabriel Grub had had time to fetch his breath, which the rapidity of his descent had for the moment taken away, he found himself in what appeared to be a large cavern, surrounded on all sides by crowds of goblins, ugly and grim; in the centre of the room, on an elevated seat, was stationed his friend of the churchyard; and close beside him stood Gabriel Grub himself, without power of motion.

"Cold tonight," said the king of the goblins, "very cold. A glass of something warm, here!"

At this command, half a dozen officious goblins, with a perpetual smile upon their faces – whom Gabriel Grub imagined to be courtiers, on that account – hastily disappeared, and presently returned with a goblet of liquid fire, which they presented to the king.

"Ah!" cried the goblin, whose cheeks and throat were transparent, as he tossed down the flame. "This warms one, indeed! Bring a bumper of the same, for Mr Grub."

It was in vain for the unfortunate sexton to protest that he was not in the habit of taking anything warm at night; one of the goblins held him while another poured the blazing liquid down his throat; the whole assembly screeched with laughter as he coughed and choked and wiped away the tears which gushed plentifully from his eyes after swallowing the burning draught.

"And now," said the king, fantastically poking the taper corner of his sugar-loaf hat into the sexton's eye, and thereby occasioning him the most exquisite pain, "and now, show the man of misery and gloom a few of the pictures from our own great storehouse."

As the goblin said this, a thick cloud which obscured the remoter end of the cavern rolled gradually away and disclosed, apparently at a great distance, a small and scantily furnished but neat and clean apartment. A crowd of little children were gathered round a bright fire, clinging to their mother's gown, and gambolling around her chair. The mother occasionally rose and drew aside the window curtain, as if to look for some expected object; a frugal meal was ready spread upon the table, and an elbow chair was placed near the fire. A knock was heard at the door: the mother opened it, and the children crowded round her and clapped their hands for joy as their father entered. He was wet and weary, and shook the snow from his garments as the children crowded round him and, seizing his cloak, hat, stick and gloves with busy zeal, ran with them from the room. Then, as he sat down to his meal before the fire, the children climbed about his knee and the mother sat by his side, and all seemed happiness and comfort.

But a change came upon the view, almost imperceptibly. The scene was altered to a small bedroom, where the fairest and youngest child lay dying; the roses had fled from his cheek, and the light from his eye; and even as the sexton looked upon him with an interest he had never felt or known before, he died. His young brothers and sisters crowded round his little bed and seized his tiny hand, so cold and heavy, but they shrunk back from its touch and looked with awe on his infant face, for calm and tranquil as it was, and sleeping in rest and peace as the beautiful child seemed to be, they saw that he was dead, and they knew that he was an angel looking down upon, and blessing them, from a bright and happy heaven.

Again the light cloud passed across the picture, and again the subject changed. The father and mother were old and helpless now, and the number of those about them was diminished more than half, but content and cheerfulness sat on every face and beamed in every eye as they crowded round the fireside and told and listened to old stories of earlier and bygone days. Slowly and peacefully, the father sank into the grave and, soon after, the sharer of all his cares and troubles followed him to a place of rest. The few who yet survived them knelt by their tomb and watered the green turf which covered it with their tears, then rose and turned away – sadly and mournfully, but not with bitter cries or despairing lamentations, for they knew that they should one day meet again; and once more they mixed with the busy world, and their content and cheerfulness were restored. The cloud settled upon the picture and concealed it from the sexton's view.

"What do you think of *that*?" said the goblin, turning his large face towards Gabriel Grub.

Gabriel murmured out something about it being very pretty, and looked somewhat ashamed as the goblin bent his fiery eyes upon him.

"*You* a miserable man!" said the goblin, in a tone of excessive contempt. "You!" He appeared disposed to add more, but indignation choked his utterance, so he lifted up one of his very pliable legs and, flourishing it above his head a little to ensure his aim, administered a good sound kick to Gabriel Grub; immediately after which, all the goblins in waiting crowded round the wretched sexton and kicked him without mercy, according to the established and invariable custom of courtiers upon earth, who kick whom royalty kicks, and hug whom royalty hugs.

"Show him some more!" said the king of the goblins.

At these words, the cloud was dispelled, and a rich and beautiful landscape was disclosed to view – there is just such another, to this day, within half a mile of the old abbey town. The sun shone from out the clear blue sky, the water sparkled beneath his rays, and the trees looked greener and the flowers more gay beneath his cheering influence. The water rippled on, with a pleasant sound; the trees rustled in the light wind that murmured among their leaves; the birds sang upon the boughs; and the lark carolled on high her welcome to the morning. Yes, it was morning – the bright, balmy morning of summer: the minutest leaf, the smallest blade of grass, was instinct with life. The ant crept forth to her daily toil, the butterfly fluttered and basked in the warm rays of the sun; myriads of insects spread their transparent wings and revelled in their brief but happy existence. Man walked forth, elated with the scene, and all was brightness and splendour.

"*You* a miserable man!" said the king of the goblins, in a more contemptuous tone than before. And again the king of the goblins gave his leg a flourish; again it descended on the shoulders of the sexton; and again the attendant goblins imitated the example of their chief.

Many a time the cloud went and came, and many a lesson it taught to Gabriel Grub – who, although his shoulders smarted with pain from the frequent applications of the goblin's feet, looked on with an interest that nothing could diminish. He saw that men who worked hard and earned their scanty bread with lives of labour were cheerful and happy, and that to the most ignorant, the sweet face of nature was a never-failing source of cheerfulness and joy. He saw those who had been delicately nurtured and tenderly brought up cheerful under privations and superior to suffering that would have crushed many of a rougher grain, because they bore within their own bosoms the materials of happiness, contentment and peace. He saw that women, the tenderest and most fragile of all God's creatures, were the oftenest superior to sorrow, adversity and distress – and he saw that it was because they bore, in their own hearts, an inexhaustible well-spring of affection and devotion. Above all, he saw that men like himself, who snarled at the mirth and cheerfulness of others, were the foulest weeds on the fair surface of the earth; and setting all the good of the world against the evil, he came to the conclusion that it was a very decent and respectable sort of world after all. No sooner had he formed it, than the cloud which closed over the last picture seemed to settle on his senses and lull him to repose. One by one, the goblins faded from his sight; and as the last one disappeared, he sunk to sleep.

The day had broken when Gabriel Grub awoke and found himself lying at full length on the flat gravestone in the churchyard with the wicker bottle lying empty by his side and his coat, spade and lantern – all well whitened by the last night's frost – scattered on the ground. The stone on which he had first seen the goblin seated stood bolt-upright before him, and the grave at which he had worked the night before was not far off. At first, he began to doubt the reality of his adventures, but the acute pain in his shoulders when he attempted to rise assured him that the kicking of the goblins was certainly not ideal. He was staggered again by observing no traces of footsteps in the snow on which the goblins had played at leap-frog with the gravestones, but he speedily accounted for this circumstance when he remembered that, being spirits, they would leave no visible impression behind them. So, Gabriel Grub got on his feet as well as he could, for the pain in his back; and brushing the frost off his coat, put it on and turned his face towards the town.

But he was an altered man, and he could not bear the thought of returning to a place where his repentance would be scoffed at and his reformation disbelieved. He hesitated for a few moments, and then turned away to wander where he might and seek his bread elsewhere.

The lantern, the spade and the wicker bottle were found, that day, in the churchyard. There were a great many speculations about the sexton's fate, at first, but it was speedily determined that he had been carried away by the goblins; and there were not wanting some very credible witnesses who had distinctly seen him whisked through the air on the back of a chestnut horse blind in one eye, with the hind-quarters of a lion and the tail of a bear. At length all this was devoutly believed; and the new sexton used to exhibit to the curious, for a trifling emolument, a good-sized piece of the church weathercock which had been accidentally kicked off by the aforesaid horse in his aerial flight and picked up by himself in the churchyard a year or two afterwards.

Unfortunately, these stories were somewhat disturbed by the unlooked-for reappearance of Gabriel Grub himself, some ten years afterwards – a ragged, contented, rheumatic old man. He told his story to the clergyman, and also to the mayor; and in course of time it began to be received as a matter of history, in which form it has continued down to this very day. The believers in the weathercock tale, having misplaced their confidence once, were not easily prevailed upon to part with it again, so they looked as wise as they could, shrugged their shoulders, touched their foreheads and murmured something about Gabriel Grub having drunk all the Hollands and then fallen asleep on the flat tombstone; and they affected to explain what he supposed he had witnessed in the goblin's cavern by saying that he had seen the world and grown wiser. But this opinion, which was by no means a popular one at any time, gradually died off; and be the matter how it may, as Gabriel Grub was afflicted with rheumatism to the end of his days, this story has at least one moral, if it teach no better one – and that is that if a man turn sulky and drink by himself at Christmas time, he may make up his mind to be not a bit the better for it: let the spirits be never so good, or let them be even as many degrees beyond proof as those which Gabriel Grub saw in the goblin's cavern.

The Story of the Bagman's Uncle*

M Y UNCLE, GENTLEMEN – said the bagman – was one of the merriest, pleasantest, cleverest fellows that ever lived. I wish you had known him, gentlemen. On second thoughts, gentlemen, I *don't* wish you had known him, for if you had, you would have been all, by this time, in the ordinary course of nature, if not dead, at all events so near it as to have taken to stopping at home and giving up company – which would have deprived me of the inestimable pleasure of addressing you at this moment. Gentlemen, I wish your fathers and mothers had known my uncle. They would have been amazingly fond of him, especially your respectable mothers – I know they would. If any two of his numerous virtues predominated over the many that adorned his character, I should say they were his mixed punch and his after-supper song. Excuse my dwelling on these melancholy recollections of departed worth: you won't see a man like my uncle every day in the week.

I have always considered it a great point in my uncle's character, gentlemen, that he was the intimate friend and companion of Tom Smart, of the great house of Bilson and Slum, Cateaton Street, City. My uncle collected for Tiggin and Welps, but for a long time he went pretty near the same journey as Tom, and the very first night they met, my uncle took a fancy for Tom, and Tom took a fancy for my uncle. They made a bet of a new hat before they had known each other half an hour who should brew the best quart of punch and drink it the quickest. My uncle was judged to have won the making, but Tom Smart beat him in the drinking by about half a salt-spoonful. They took another quart apiece to drink each other's health in, and were staunch friends ever afterwards. There's a destiny in these things, gentlemen: we can't help it.

In personal appearance, my uncle was a trifle shorter than the middle size; he was a thought stouter too than the ordinary run of people, and perhaps his face might be a shade redder. He had the jolliest face you ever saw, gentlemen: something like Punch, with a handsomer nose and chin; his eyes were always twinkling and sparkling with good humour; and a smile – not one of your unmeaning wooden grins, but a real, merry, hearty, good-tempered smile – was perpetually on his countenance. He was pitched out of his gig once, and knocked head first against a milestone. There he lay, stunned, and so cut about the face with some gravel which had been heaped up alongside it that, to use my uncle's own strong expression, if his mother could have revisited the earth, she wouldn't have known him. Indeed, when I come to think of the matter, gentlemen, I feel pretty sure she wouldn't, for she died when my uncle was two years and seven months old, and I think it's very likely that, even without the gravel, his top boots would have puzzled the good lady not a little – to say nothing of his jolly red face. However, there he lay, and I have heard my uncle say, many a time, that the man said who picked him up that he was smiling as merrily as if he had tumbled out for a treat, and that after they had bled him, the first faint glimmerings of returning animation were his jumping up in bed, bursting out into a loud laugh, kissing the young woman who held the basin and demanding a mutton chop and a pickled walnut. He was very fond of pickled walnuts, gentlemen. He said he always found that, taken without vinegar, they relished the beer.

My uncle's great journey was in the fall of the leaf, at which time he collected debts and took orders in the north, going from London to Edinburgh, from Edinburgh to Glasgow, from Glasgow back to Edinburgh, and thence to London by the smack. You are to understand that his second visit to Edinburgh was for his own pleasure. He used to go back for a week, just to look up his old friends; and what with breakfasting with this one, lunching with that, dining with a third and supping with another, a pretty tight week he used to make of it. I don't know whether any of you, gentlemen, ever partook of a real substantial hospitable Scotch breakfast and then went out to a slight lunch of a bushel of oysters, a dozen or so of bottled ale and a noggin or two of whiskey to close up with. If you ever did, you will agree with me that it requires a pretty strong head to go out to dinner and supper afterwards.

But, bless your hearts and eyebrows, all this sort of thing was nothing to my uncle! He was so well seasoned that it was mere child's play. I have heard him say that he could see the Dundee people out, any day, and walk home afterwards without staggering; and yet the Dundee people have as strong heads and as strong punch, gentlemen, as you are likely to meet with between the poles. I have heard of a Glasgow man and a Dundee man drinking against each other for fifteen hours at a sitting. They were both suffocated, as nearly as could be ascertained, at the same moment, but with this trifling exception, gentlemen: they were not a bit the worse for it.

One night, within four-and-twenty hours of the time when he had settled to take shipping for London, my uncle supped at the house of a very old friend of his, a bailie MacSomething and four syllables after it, who lived in the old town of Edinburgh. There were the bailie's wife, and the bailie's three daughters and the bailie's grown-up son, and three or four stout, bushy-eyebrowed, canny old Scotch fellows that the bailie had got together to do honour to my uncle and help to make merry. It was a glorious supper. There were kippered salmon and finnan-haddocks, and a lamb's head and a haggis – a celebrated Scotch dish, gentlemen, which my uncle used to say always looked to him, when it came to table, very much like a cupid's stomach – and a great many other things besides that I forget the names of, but very good things notwithstanding. The lassies were pretty and agreeable; the bailie's wife was one of the best creatures that ever lived; and my uncle was in thoroughly good cue. The consequence of which was that the young ladies tittered and giggled, and the old lady laughed out loud, and the bailie and the other old fellows roared till they were red in the face the whole mortal time. I don't quite recollect how many tumblers of whisky toddy each man drank after supper, but this I know: that about one o'clock in the morning, the bailie's grown-up son became insensible while attempting the first verse of 'Willie Brew'd a Peck o' Maut' – and he having been, for an hour before, the only other man visible above the mahogany, it occurred to my uncle that it was almost time to think about going, especially as drinking had set in at seven o'clock, in order that he might get home at a decent hour. But thinking it might not be quite polite to go just then, my uncle voted himself into the chair, mixed another glass, rose to propose his own health, addressed himself in a neat and complimentary speech and drank the toast with great enthusiasm. Still nobody woke; so my uncle took a little drop more – neat this time, to prevent the toddy from disagreeing with him – and, laying violent hands on his hat, sallied forth into the street.

It was a wild gusty night when my uncle closed the bailie's door and, settling his hat firmly on his head, to prevent the wind from taking it, thrust his hands into his pockets and, looking upwards, took a short survey of the state of the weather. The clouds were drifting over the moon at their giddiest speed, at one time wholly obscuring her, at another suffering her to burst forth in full splendour and shed her light on all the objects around, anon driving over her again with increased velocity and shrouding everything in darkness. "Really, this won't do," said my uncle, addressing himself to the weather, as if he felt himself personally offended. "This is not at all the kind of thing for my voyage. It will not do, at any price," said my uncle very impressively. Having repeated this several times, he recovered his balance with some difficulty – for he was rather giddy with looking up into the sky so long – and walked merrily on.

The bailie's house was in the Canongate, and my uncle was going to the other end of Leith Walk, rather better than a mile's journey. On either side of him, there shot up against the dark sky tall, gaunt, straggling houses with time-stained fronts, and windows that seemed to have shared the lot of eyes in mortals and to have grown dim and sunken with age. Six, seven, eight storeys high were the houses – storey piled above storey, as children build with cards – throwing their dark shadows over the roughly paved road and making the dark night darker. A few oil lamps were scattered at long distances, but they only served to mark the dirty entrance to some narrow close or to show where a common stair communicated, by steep and intricate windings, with the various flats above. Glancing at all these things with the air of a man who had seen them too often before to think them worthy of much notice now, my uncle walked up the middle of the street with a thumb in each waistcoat pocket, indulging from time to time in various snatches of song, chaunted forth with such goodwill and spirit that the quiet honest folk started from their first sleep and lay trembling in bed till the sound died away in the distance – when, satisfying themselves that it was only some drunken ne'er-do-well finding his way home, they covered themselves up warm and fell asleep again.

I am particular in describing how my uncle walked up the middle of the street with his thumbs in his waistcoat pockets, gentlemen, because, as he often used to say (and with great reason too) there is nothing at all extraordinary in this story, unless you distinctly understand at the beginning that he was not by any means of a marvellous or romantic turn.

Gentlemen, my uncle walked on with his thumbs in his waistcoat pockets, taking the middle of the street to himself and singing now a verse of a love song and then a verse of a drinking one – and, when he was tired of both, whistling melodiously – until he reached the North Bridge, which at this point connects the old and new towns of Edinburgh. Here he stopped for a minute to look at the strange irregular clusters of lights piled one above the other and twinkling afar off so high that they looked like stars gleaming from the castle walls on the one side and the Calton Hill on the other, as if they illuminated veritable castles in the air, while the old picturesque town slept heavily on in gloom and darkness below, its palace and chapel of Holyrood guarded day and night, as a friend of my uncle's used to say, by old Arthur's Seat, towering surly and dark, like some gruff genius, over the ancient city he has watched so long. I say, gentlemen, my uncle stopped here for a minute to look about him, and then, paying a compliment to the weather which had a little cleared up, though the moon was sinking, walked on again as royally as before, keeping the middle of the road with great dignity and looking as if he would very much like to meet with somebody who would dispute possession of it with him. There was nobody at all disposed to contest the point, as it happened, and so on he went, with his thumbs in his waistcoat pockets, like a lamb.

When my uncle reached the end of Leith Walk, he had to cross a pretty large piece of waste ground which separated him from a short street which he had to turn down to go direct to his lodging. Now, in this piece of waste ground, there was at that time an enclosure belonging to some wheelwright who contracted with the Post Office for the purchase of old worn-out mail coaches, and my uncle, being very fond of coaches – old, young or middle-aged – all at once took it into his head to step out of his road for no other purpose than to peep between the palings at these mails – about a dozen of which he remembered to have seen crowded together in a very forlorn and dismantled state inside. My uncle was a very enthusiastic, emphatic sort of person, gentlemen; so, finding that he could not obtain a good peep between the palings, he got over them and, sitting himself quietly down on an old axle tree, began to contemplate the mail coaches with a deal of gravity.

There might be a dozen of them, or there might be more – my uncle was never quite certain on this point, and being a man of very scrupulous veracity about numbers, didn't like to say – but there they stood, all huddled together in the most desolate condition imaginable. The doors had been torn from their hinges and removed; the linings had been stripped off: only a shred hanging here and there by a rusty nail; the lamps were gone, the poles had long since vanished, the ironwork was rusty, the paint was worn away; the wind whistled through the chinks in the bare woodwork; and the rain, which had collected on the roofs, fell drop by drop into the insides with a hollow and melancholy sound. They were the decaying skeletons of departed mails, and in that lonely place, at that time of night, they looked chill and dismal.

My uncle rested his head upon his hands and thought of the busy bustling people who had rattled about, years before, in the old coaches and were now as silent and changed; he thought of the numbers of people to whom one of those crazy, mouldering vehicles had borne night after night for many years and through all weathers, the anxiously expected intelligence, the eagerly looked-for remittance, the promised assurance of health and safety, the sudden announcement of sickness and death. The merchant, the lover, the wife, the widow, the mother, the schoolboy, the very child who tottered to the door at the postman's knock – how had they all looked forward to the arrival of the old coach. And where were they all now!

Gentlemen, my uncle used to *say* that he thought all this at the time, but I rather suspect he learnt it out of some book afterwards, for he distinctly stated that he fell into a kind of doze as he sat on the old axle tree looking at the decayed mail coaches, and that he was suddenly awakened by some deep church bell striking two. Now, my uncle was never a fast thinker, and if he had thought all these things, I am quite certain it would have taken him till full half-past two o'clock at the very least. I am therefore decidedly of opinion, gentlemen, that my uncle fell into the kind of doze without having thought about anything at all.

Be this as it may, a church bell struck two. My uncle woke, rubbed his eyes and jumped up in astonishment.

In one instant after the clock struck two, the whole of this deserted and quiet spot had become a scene of most extraordinary life and animation. The mail-coach doors were on their hinges, the lining was replaced, the ironwork was as good as new, the paint was restored, the lamps were alight, cushions and great coats were on every coach box, porters were thrusting parcels into every boot, guards were stowing away letter bags, hostlers were dashing pails of water against the renovated wheels; numbers of men were rushing about, fixing poles into every coach; passengers arrived, portmanteaus were handed up, horses were put to; in short, it was perfectly clear that every mail there was to be off directly. Gentlemen, my uncle opened his eyes so wide at all this that, to the very last moment of his life, he used to wonder how it fell out that he had ever been able to shut 'em again.

"Now then!" said a voice, as my uncle felt a hand on his shoulder. "You're booked for one inside. You'd better get in."

"*I* booked!" said my uncle, turning round.

"Yes, certainly."

My uncle, gentlemen, could say nothing: he was so very much astonished. The queerest thing of all was that although there was such a crowd of persons, and although fresh faces were pouring in every moment, there was no telling where they came from. They seemed to start up in some strange manner from the ground or the air, and disappear in the same way. When a porter had put his luggage in the coach and received his fare, he turned round and was gone; and before my uncle had well begun to wonder what had become of him, half a dozen fresh ones started up and staggered along under the weight of parcels which seemed big enough to crush them. The passengers were all dressed so oddly too! Large, broad-skirted laced coats with great cuffs and no collars – and wigs, gentlemen, great formal wigs with a tie behind. My uncle could make nothing of it.

"Now, *are* you going to get in?" said the person who had addressed my uncle before. He was dressed as a mail guard, with a wig on his head and most enormous cuffs to his coat, and had a lantern in one hand and a huge blunderbuss in the other, which he was going to stow away in his little arm-chest. "*Are* you going to get in, Jack Martin?" said the guard, holding the lantern to my uncle's face.

"Hallo!" said my uncle, falling back a step or two. "That's familiar!"

"It's so on the waybill," replied the guard.

"Isn't there a 'Mister' before it?" said my uncle. For he felt, gentlemen, that for a guard he didn't know, to call him Jack Martin was a liberty which the Post Office wouldn't have sanctioned if they had known it.

"No, there is not," rejoined the guard coolly.

"Is the fare paid?" enquired my uncle.

"Of course it is," rejoined the guard.

"It is, is it?" said my uncle. "Then here goes! Which coach?"

"This," said the guard, pointing to an old-fashioned Edinburgh and London Mail which had the steps down and the door open. "Stop! Here are the other passengers. Let them get in first."

As the guard spoke, there all at once appeared, right in front of my uncle, a young gentleman in a powdered wig and a sky-blue coat trimmed with silver, made very full and broad in the skirts, which were lined with buckram. Tiggin and Welps were in the printed-calico and waistcoat-piece line, gentlemen, so my uncle knew all the materials at once. He wore knee breeches and a kind of leggings rolled up over his silk stockings, and shoes with buckles; he had ruffles at his wrists, a three-cornered hat on his head and a long taper sword by his side. The flaps of his waistcoat came halfway down his thighs, and the ends of his cravat reached to his waist. He stalked gravely to the coach door, pulled off his hat and held it above his head at arm's length, cocking his little finger in the air at the same time, as some affected people do when they take a cup of tea. Then he drew his feet together and made a low, grave bow, and then put out his left hand. My uncle was just going to step forward and shake it heartily, when he perceived that these attentions were directed not towards him, but to a young lady who just then appeared at the foot of the steps, attired in an old-fashioned green-velvet dress with a long waist and stomacher. She had no bonnet on her head, gentlemen, which was muffled in a black silk hood, but she looked round for an instant as she prepared to get into the coach – and such a beautiful face as she disclosed my uncle had never seen, not even in a picture. She got into the coach, holding up her dress with one hand; and as my uncle always said with a round oath when he told the story, he wouldn't have believed it possible that legs and feet could have been brought to such a state of perfection unless he had seen them with his own eyes.

But in this one glimpse of the beautiful face, my uncle saw that the young lady cast an imploring look upon him, and that she appeared terrified and distressed. He noticed, too, that the young fellow in the powdered wig, notwithstanding his show of gallantry – which was all very fine and grand – clasped her tight by the wrist when she got in, and followed himself immediately afterwards. An uncommonly ill-looking fellow in a close brown wig and a plum-coloured suit, wearing a very large sword and boots up to his hips, belonged to the party; and when he sat himself down next to the young lady, who shrunk into a corner at his approach, my uncle was confirmed in his original impression that something dark and mysterious was going forward – or, as he always said himself, that "there was a screw loose somewhere". It's quite surprising how quickly he made up his mind to help the lady at any peril, if she needed help.

"Death and lightning!" exclaimed the young gentleman, laying his hand upon his sword as my uncle entered the coach.

"Blood and thunder!" roared the other gentleman. With this, he whipped his sword out and made a lunge at my uncle without further ceremony. My uncle had no weapon about him, but with great dexterity he snatched the ill-looking gentleman's three-cornered hat from his head and, receiving the point of his sword right through the crown, squeezed the sides together and held it tight.

"Pink him behind!" cried the ill-looking gentleman to his companion, as he struggled to regain his sword.

"He had better not," cried my uncle, displaying the heel of one of his shoes in a threatening manner. "I'll kick his brains out, if he has any, or fracture his skull if he hasn't." Exerting all his strength at this moment, my uncle wrenched the ill-looking man's sword from his grasp and flung it clean out of the coach window – upon which, the younger gentleman vociferated "Death and lightning!" again and laid his hand upon the hilt of his sword in a very fierce manner, but didn't draw it. Perhaps, gentlemen, as my uncle used to say with a smile, perhaps he was afraid of alarming the lady.

"Now, gentlemen," said my uncle, taking his seat deliberately, "I don't want to have any death, with or without lightning, in a lady's presence, and we have had quite blood and thundering enough for one journey – so, if you please, we'll sit in our places like quiet insides. Here, guard, pick up that gentleman's carving knife."

As quickly as my uncle said the words, the guard appeared at the coach window with the gentleman's sword in his hand. He held up his lantern and looked earnestly in my uncle's face as he handed it in – when, by its light, my uncle saw to his great surprise that an immense crowd of mail-coach guards swarmed round the window, every one of whom had his eyes earnestly fixed upon him too. He had never seen such a sea of white faces, red bodies and earnest eyes in all his born days.

"This is the strangest sort of thing I ever had anything to do with," thought my uncle. "Allow me to return you your hat, sir."

The ill-looking gentleman received his three-cornered hat in silence, looked at the hole in the middle with an enquiring air and finally stuck it on the top of his wig, with a solemnity the effect of which was a trifle impaired by his sneezing violently at the moment, and jerking it off again.

"All right!" cried the guard with the lantern, mounting into his little seat behind. Away they went. My uncle peeped out of the coach window as they emerged from the yard and observed that the other mails, with coachmen, guards, horses and passengers complete, were driving round and round in circles, at a slow trot of about five miles an hour. My uncle burned with indignation, gentlemen. As a commercial man, he felt that the mail bags were not to be trifled with, and he resolved to memorialize the Post Office on the subject the very instant he reached London.

At present, however, his thought were occupied with the young lady who sat in the farthest corner of the coach with her face muffled closely in her hood, the gentleman with the sky-blue coat sitting opposite to her, the other man in the plum-coloured suit by her side, and both watching her intently. If she so much as rustled the folds of her hood, he could hear the ill-looking man clap his hand upon his sword, and could tell by the other's breathing (it was so dark he couldn't see his face) that he was looking as big as if he were going to devour her at a mouthful. This roused my uncle more and more, and he resolved, come what come might, to see the end of it. He had a great admiration for bright eyes and sweet faces, and pretty legs and feet – in short, he was fond of the whole sex. It runs in our family, gentlemen: so am I.

Many were the devices which my uncle practised to attract the lady's attention – or at all events to engage the mysterious gentlemen in conversation. They were all in vain: the gentlemen wouldn't talk, and the lady didn't dare. He thrust his head out of the coach window at intervals and bawled out to know why they didn't go faster. But he called till he was hoarse: nobody paid the least attention to him. He leant back in the coach and thought of the beautiful face, and the feet and legs. This answered better: it whiled away the time and kept him from wondering where he was going, and how it was that he found himself in such an odd situation. Not that this would have worried him much anyway: he was a mighty free-and-easy, roving, devil-may-care sort of person, was my uncle, gentlemen.

All of a sudden the coach stopped. "Hallo!" said my uncle. "What's in the wind now?"

"Alight here," said the guard, letting down the steps.

"Here!" cried my uncle.

"Here," rejoined the guard.

"I'll do nothing of the sort," said my uncle.

"Very well, then stop where you are," said the guard.

"I will," said my uncle.

"Do," said the guard.

The other passengers had regarded this colloquy with great attention, and finding that my uncle was determined not to alight, the younger man squeezed past him to hand the lady out. At this moment, the ill-looking man was inspecting the hole in the crown of his three-cornered hat. As the young lady brushed past, she dropped one of her gloves into my uncle's hand and softly whispered, with her lips – so close to his face that he felt her warm breath on his nose – the single word "Help!" Gentlemen, my uncle leapt out of the coach at once, with such violence that it rocked on the springs again.

"Oh! You've thought better of it, have you?" said the guard when he saw my uncle standing on the ground.

My uncle looked at the guard for a few seconds, in some doubt whether it wouldn't be better to wrench his blunderbuss from him, fire it in the face of the man with the big sword, knock the rest of the company over the head with the stock, snatch up the young lady and go off in the smoke. On second thoughts, however, he abandoned this plan as being a shade too melodramatic in the execution and followed the two mysterious men – who, keeping the lady between them, were now entering an old house in front of which the coach had stopped. They turned into the passage, and my uncle followed.

Of all the ruinous and desolate places my uncle had ever beheld, this was the most so. It looked as if it had once been a large house of entertainment, but the roof had fallen in in many places, and the stairs were steep, rugged and broken. There was a huge fireplace in the room into which they walked, and the chimney was blackened with smoke, but no warm blaze lighted it up now. The white feathery dust of burnt wood was still strewed over the hearth, but the stove was cold, and all was dark and gloomy.

"Well," said my uncle as he looked about him, "a mail travelling at the rate of six miles and a half an hour, and stopping for an indefinite time at such a hole as this, is rather an irregular sort of proceeding, I fancy. This shall be made known. I'll write to the papers."

My uncle said this in a pretty loud voice, and in an open, unreserved sort of manner, with the view of engaging the two strangers in conversation if he could. But neither of them took any more notice of him than whispering to each other and scowling at him as they did so. The lady was at the farther end of the room, and once she ventured to wave her hand, as if beseeching my uncle's assistance.

At length the two strangers advanced a little, and the conversation began in earnest.

"You don't know this is a private room, I suppose, fellow?" said the gentleman in sky-blue.

"No, I do not, fellow," rejoined my uncle. "Only, if this is a private room specially ordered for the occasion, I should think the public room must be a *very* comfortable one" – with this my uncle sat himself down in a high-backed chair and took such an accurate measure of the gentleman with his eyes that Tiggin and Welps could have supplied him with printed calico for a suit, and not an inch too much or too little, from that estimate alone.

"Quit this room," said both the men together, grasping their swords.

"Eh?" said my uncle, not at all appearing to comprehend their meaning.

"Quit the room, or you are a dead man," said the ill-looking fellow with the large sword, drawing it at the same time and flourishing it in the air.

"Down with him!" cried the gentleman in sky-blue, drawing his sword also, and falling back two or three yards. "Down with him!" The lady gave a loud scream.

Now, my uncle was always remarkable for great boldness and great presence of mind. All the time that he had appeared so indifferent to what was going on, he had been looking slyly about for some missile or weapon of defence, and at the very instant when the swords were drawn, he espied, standing in the chimney corner, an old basket-hilted rapier in a rusty scabbard. At one bound, my uncle caught it in his hand, drew it, flourished it gallantly above his head, called aloud to the lady to keep out of the way, hurled the chair at the man in sky-blue and the scabbard at the man in plum colour, and taking advantage of the confusion, fell upon them both, pell-mell.

Gentlemen, there is an old story – none the worse for being true – regarding a fine young Irish gentleman who, being asked if he could play the fiddle, replied he had no doubt he could, but he couldn't exactly say for certain, because he had never tried. This is not inapplicable to my uncle and his fencing. He had never had a sword in his hand before, except once when he played Richard III at a private theatre – upon which occasion it was arranged with Richmond that he was to be run through from behind without showing fight at all. But here he was, cutting and slashing with two experienced swordsmen – thrusting and guarding and poking and slicing, and acquitting himself in the most manful and dextrous manner possible, although up to that time he had never been aware that he had the least notion of the science. It only shows how true the old saying is: that a man never knows what he can do till he tries, gentlemen.

The noise of the combat was terrific, each of the three combatants swearing like troopers, and their swords clashing with as much noise as if all the knives and steels in Newport market were rattling together at the same time. When it was at its very height, the lady (to encourage my uncle, most probably) withdrew her hood entirely from her face and disclosed a countenance of such dazzling beauty that he would have fought against fifty men to win one smile from it and die. He had done wonders before, but now he began to powder away like a raving-mad giant.

At this very moment, the gentleman in sky-blue, turning round and seeing the young lady with her face uncovered, vented an exclamation of rage and jealousy, and turning his weapon against her beautiful bosom, pointed a thrust at her heart, which caused my uncle to utter a cry of apprehension that made the building ring. The lady stepped lightly aside and, snatching the young man's sword from his hand before he had recovered his balance, drove him to the wall and, running it through him and the panelling up to the very hilt, pinned him there hard and fast. It was a splendid example. My uncle, with a loud shout of triumph and a strength that was irresistible, made his adversary retreat in the same direction and, plunging the old rapier into the very centre of a large red flower in the pattern of his waistcoat, nailed him beside his friend; there they both stood, gentlemen, jerking their arms and legs about in agony, like the toy-shop figures that are moved by a piece of packthread. My uncle always said, afterwards, that this was one of the surest means he knew of for disposing of an enemy, but it was liable to one objection on the ground of expense, inasmuch as it involved the loss of a sword for every man disabled.

"The mail! the mail!" cried the lady, running up to my uncle and throwing her beautiful arms round his neck. "We may yet escape."

"*May*!" cried my uncle. "Why, my dear, there's nobody else to kill, is there?" My uncle was rather disappointed, gentlemen, for he thought a little, quiet bit of love-making would be agreeable after the slaughtering, if it were only to change the subject.

"We have not an instant to lose here," said the young lady. "He" – pointing to the young gentleman in sky-blue – "is the only son of the powerful Marquess of Filletoville."

"Well, then, my dear, I'm afraid he'll never come to the title," said my uncle, looking coolly at the young gentleman as he stood fixed up against the wall in the cockchafer fashion I have described. "You have cut off the entail, my love."

"I have been torn from my home and friends by these villains," said the young lady, her features glowing with indignation. "That wretch would have married me by violence in another hour."

"Confound his impudence!" said my uncle, bestowing a very contemptuous look on the dying heir of Filletoville.

"As you may guess from what you have seen," said the young lady, "the party were prepared to murder me if I appealed to anyone for assistance. If their accomplices find us here, we are lost. Two minutes hence may be too late! The mail!" With these words, overpowered by her feelings and the exertion of sticking the young Marquess of Filletoville, she sunk into my uncle's arms. My uncle caught her up and bore her to the house door. There stood the mail, with four long-tailed, flowing-maned black horses ready-harnessed – but no coachman, no guard, no hostler even at the horses' heads.

Gentlemen, I hope I do no injustice to my uncle's memory when I express my opinion that, although he was a bachelor, he *had* held some ladies in his arms before this time – I believe, indeed, that he had rather a habit of kissing barmaids, and I know that in one or two instances he had been seen by credible witnesses to hug a landlady in a very perceptible manner. I mention the circumstance to show what a very uncommon sort of person this beautiful young lady must have been to have affected my uncle in the way she did; he used to say that as her long dark hair trailed over his arm and her beautiful dark eyes fixed themselves upon his face when she recovered, he felt so strange and nervous that his legs trembled beneath him. But who can look in a sweet soft pair of dark eyes without feeling queer? *I* can't, gentlemen. I am afraid to look at some eyes I know – and that's the truth of it.

"You will never leave me," murmured the young lady.

"Never," said my uncle. And he meant it too.

"My dear preserver!" exclaimed the young lady. "My dear, kind, brave preserver!"

"Don't," said my uncle, interrupting her.

"Why?" enquired the young lady.

"Because your mouth looks so beautiful when you speak," rejoined my uncle, "that I'm afraid I shall be rude enough to kiss it."

The young lady put up her hand as if to caution my uncle not to do so and said – no, she didn't say anything: she smiled. When you are looking at a pair of the most delicious lips in the world and see them gently break into a roguish smile – if you are very near them and nobody else by – you cannot better testify your admiration of their beautiful form and colour than by kissing them at once. My uncle did so, and I honour him for it.

"Hark!" cried the young lady, starting. "The noise of wheels and horses!"

"So it is," said my uncle, listening. He had a good ear for wheels and the trampling of hoofs, but there appeared to be so many horses and carriages rattling towards them from a distance that it was impossible to form a guess at their number. The sound was like that of fifty breaks with six blood cattle in each.

"We are pursued!" cried the young lady, clasping her hands. "We are pursued. I have no hope but in you!"

There was such an expression of terror in her beautiful face that my uncle made up his mind at once. He lifted her into the coach, told her not to be frightened, pressed his lips to hers once more and then, advising her to draw up the window to keep the cold air out, mounted to the box.

"Stay, love," cried the young lady.

"What's the matter?" said my uncle from the coach box.

"I want to speak to you," said the young lady. "Only a word. Only one word, dearest."

"Must I get down?" enquired my uncle. The lady made no answer, but she smiled again. Such a smile, gentlemen! It beat the other one all to nothing. My uncle descended from his perch in a twinkling.

"What is it, my dear?" said my uncle, looking in at the coach window. The lady happened to bend forward at the same time, and my uncle thought she looked more beautiful than she had done yet. He was very close to her just then, gentlemen, so he really ought to know.

"What is it, dear?" said my uncle.

"Will you never love anyone but me – never marry anyone beside?" said the young lady.

My uncle swore a great oath that he never would marry anybody else, and the young lady drew in her head and pulled up the window. He jumped upon the box, squared his elbows, adjusted the ribands, seized the whip which lay on the roof, gave one flick to the off leader and away went the four long-tailed, flowing-maned black horses, at fifteen good English miles an hour, with the old mail coach behind them. Whew! How they tore along!

The noise behind grew louder. The faster the old mail went, the faster came the pursuers – men, horses, dogs were leagued in the pursuit. The noise was frightful, but above all rose the voice of the young lady, urging my uncle on and shrieking, "Faster! Faster!"

They whirled past the dark trees as feathers would be swept before a hurricane. Houses, gates, churches, haystacks, objects of every kind they shot by, with a velocity and noise like roaring waters suddenly let loose. Still the noise of pursuit grew louder, and still my uncle could hear the young lady wildly screaming, "Faster! Faster!"

My uncle plied whip and rein, and the horses flew onward till they were white with foam – and yet the noise behind increased, and yet the young lady cried, "Faster! Faster!" My uncle gave a loud stamp on the boot in the energy of the moment and... found that it was grey morning, and he was sitting in the wheelwright's yard on the box of an old Edinburgh mail, shivering with the cold and wet and stamping his feet to warm them! He got down and looked eagerly inside for the beautiful young lady. Alas! There was neither door nor seat to the coach. It was a mere shell.

Of course, my uncle knew very well that there was some mystery in the matter, and that everything had passed exactly as he used to relate it. He remained staunch to the great oath he had sworn to the beautiful young lady, refusing several eligible landladies on her account and dying a bachelor at last. He always said what a curious thing it was that he should have found out by such a mere accident as his clambering over the palings that the ghosts of mail coaches and horses, guards, coachmen and passengers were in the habit of making journeys regularly every night. He used to add that he believed he was the only living person who had ever been taken as a passenger on one of these excursions. And I think he was right, gentlemen – at least I never heard of any other.

The Baron of Grogzwig*

THE BARON VON KOËLDWETHOUT, of Grogzwig in Germany, was as likely a young baron as you would wish to see. I needn't say that he lived in a castle, because that's of course – neither need I say that he lived in an old castle, for what German baron ever lived in a new one? There were many strange circumstances connected with this venerable building, among which not the least startling and mysterious were that when the wind blew it rumbled in the chimneys, or even howled among the trees in the neighbouring forest, and that when the moon shone, she found her way through certain small loopholes in the wall and actually made some parts of the wide halls and galleries quite light, while she left others in gloomy shadow. I believe that one of the baron's ancestors, being short of money, had inserted a dagger in a gentleman who called one night to ask his way, and it *was* supposed that these miraculous occurrences took place in consequence. And yet I hardly know how that could have been, either, because the baron's ancestor, who was an amiable man, felt very sorry afterwards for having been so rash and, laying violent hands upon a quantity of stone and timber which belonged to a weaker baron, built a chapel as an apology, and so took a receipt from Heaven, in full of all demands.

Talking of the baron's ancestor puts me in mind of the baron's great claims to respect on the score of his pedigree. I am afraid to say, I am sure, how many ancestors the baron had, but I know that he had a great many more than any other man of his time – and I only wish that he had lived in these latter days, that he might have done more. It is a very hard thing upon the great men of past centuries that they should have come into the world so soon, because a man who was born three or four hundred years ago cannot reasonably be expected to have had as many relations before him as a man who is born now. The last man, whoever he is – and he may be a cobbler or some low vulgar dog for aught we know – will have a longer pedigree than the greatest nobleman now alive; and I contend that this is not fair.

Well, but the Baron Von Koëldwethout of Grogzwig! He was a fine swarthy fellow, with dark hair and large moustaches, who rode a-hunting in clothes of Lincoln green, with russet boots on his feet and a bugle slung over his shoulder like the guard of a long stage. When he blew his bugle, four-and-twenty other gentlemen of inferior rank, in Lincoln green a little coarser and russet boots with a little thicker soles, turned out directly, and away galloped the whole train, with spears in their hands like lacquered area railings, to hunt down the boars, or perhaps encounter a bear – in which latter case the baron killed him first and greased his whiskers with him afterwards.

This was a merry life for the Baron of Grogzwig, and a merrier still for the baron's retainers, who drank Rhine wine every night till they fell under the table, and then had the bottles on the floor and called for pipes. Never were such jolly, roistering, rollicking, merry-making blades as the jovial crew of Grogzwig.

But the pleasures of the table, or the pleasures of under the table, require a little variety – especially when the same five-and-twenty people sit daily down to the same board to discuss the same subjects and tell the same stories. The baron grew weary and wanted excitement. He took to quarrelling with his gentlemen, and tried kicking two or three of them every day after dinner. This was a pleasant change at first, but it became monotonous after a week or so, and the baron felt quite out of sorts, and cast about in despair for some new amusement.

One night, after a day's sport in which he had outdone Nimrod or Gillingwater* and slaughtered "another fine bear" and brought him home in triumph, the Baron Von Koëldwethout sat moodily at the head of his table, eyeing the smoky roof of the hall with a discontented aspect. He swallowed huge bumpers of wine, but the more he swallowed, the more he frowned. The gentlemen who had been honoured with the dangerous distinction of sitting on his right and left imitated him to a miracle in the drinking and frowned at each other.

"I will!" cried the baron suddenly, smiting the table with his right hand and twirling his moustache with his left. "Fill to the Lady of Grogzwig!"

The four-and-twenty Lincoln greens turned pale, with the exception of their four-and-twenty noses, which were unchangeable.

"I said to the Lady of Grogzwig," repeated the baron, looking round the board.

"To the Lady of Grogzwig!" shouted the Lincoln greens – and down their four-and-twenty throats went four-and-twenty imperial pints of such rare old hock that they smacked their eight-and-forty lips and winked again.

"The fair daughter of the Baron Von Swillenhausen," said Koëldwethout, condescending to explain. "We will demand her in marriage of her father ere the sun goes down tomorrow. If he refuse our suit, we will cut off his nose."

A hoarse murmur arose from the company: every man touched first the hilt of his sword and then the tip of his nose, with appalling significance.

What a pleasant thing filial piety is to contemplate! If the daughter of the Baron Von Swillenhausen had pleaded a pre-occupied heart or fallen at her father's feet and corned them in salt tears, or only fainted away and complimented the old gentleman in frantic ejaculations, the odds are a hundred to one but Swillenhausen's Castle would have been turned out at window, or rather the baron turned out at window and the castle demolished. The damsel held her peace, however, when an early messenger bore request of Von Koëldwethout next morning, and modestly retired to her chamber from the casement of which she watched the coming of the suitor and his retinue. She was no sooner assured that the horseman with the large moustaches was her proffered husband than she hastened to her father's presence and expressed her readiness to sacrifice herself to secure his peace. The venerable baron caught his child to his arms and shed a wink of joy.

There was great feasting at the castle that day. The four-and-twenty Lincoln greens of Von Koëldwethout exchanged vows of eternal friendship with twelve Lincoln greens of Von Swillenhausen and promised the old baron that they would drink his wine "Till all was blue" – meaning, probably, until their whole countenances had acquired the same tint as their noses. Everybody slapped everybody else's back when the time for parting came, and the Baron Von Koëldwethout and his followers rode gaily home.

For six mortal weeks the bears and boars had a holiday. The houses of Koëldwethout and Swillenhausen were united: the spears rusted, and the baron's bugle grew hoarse for lack of blowing.

Those were great times for the four-and-twenty – but, alas! their high and palmy days had taken boots to themselves and were already walking off.

"My dear," said the baroness.

"My love," said the baron.

"Those coarse, noisy men…"

"Which, ma'am?" said the baron, starting.

The baroness pointed, from the window at which they stood, to the courtyard beneath, where the unconscious Lincoln greens were taking a copious stirrup-cup preparatory to issuing forth after a boar or two.

"My hunting train, ma'am," said the baron.

"Disband them, love," murmured the baroness.

"Disband them!" cried the baron in amazement.

"To please me, love," replied the baroness.

"To please the Devil, ma'am," answered the baron.

Whereupon the baroness uttered a great cry and swooned away at the baron's feet.

What could the baron do? He called for the lady's maid and roared for the doctor – and then, rushing into the yard, kicked the two Lincoln greens who were the most used to it and, cursing the others all round, bade them go… But never mind where. I don't know the German for it, or I would put it delicately that way.

It is not for me to say by what means, or by what degrees, some wives manage to keep down some husbands as they do, although

I may have my private opinion on the subject and may think that
no Member of Parliament ought to be married, inasmuch as three
married members out of every four must vote according to their
wives' consciences (if there be such things) and not according
to their own. All I need say, just now, is that the Baroness Von
Koëldwethout somehow or other acquired great control over the
Baron Von Koëldwethout, and that – little by little, and bit by bit,
and day by day, and year by year – the baron got the worst of some
disputed question, or was slyly unhorsed from some old hobby;
and that, by the time he was a fat hearty fellow of forty-eight or
thereabouts, he had no feasting, no revelry, no hunting train and
no hunting – nothing, in short, that he liked or used to have; and
that, although he was as fierce as a lion and as bold as brass, he
was decidedly snubbed and put down by his own lady, in his own
castle of Grogzwig.

Nor was this the whole extent of the baron's misfortunes. About
a year after his nuptials, there came into the world a lusty young
baron, in whose honour a great many fireworks were let off and
a great many dozens of wine drunk; but next year there came a
young baroness, and next year another young baron, and so on,
every year, either a baron or baroness (and one year both together),
until the baron found himself the father of a small family of twelve.
Upon every one of these anniversaries the venerable Baroness Von
Swillenhausen was nervously sensitive for the well-being of her
child the Baroness Von Koëldwethout; and although it was not
found that the good lady ever did anything material towards con-
tributing to her child's recovery, still she made it a point of duty to
be as nervous as possible at the castle of Grogzwig, and to divide
her time between moral observations on the baron's housekeeping
and bewailing the hard lot of her unhappy daughter. And if the
Baron of Grogzwig, a little hurt and irritated at this, took heart and
ventured to suggest that his wife was at least no worse off than the
wives of other barons, the Baroness Von Swillenhausen begged all
persons to take notice that nobody but she sympathized with her
dear daughter's sufferings – upon which her relations and friends
remarked that to be sure she did cry a great deal more than her

son-in-law, and that, if there were a hard-hearted brute alive, it was that Baron of Grogzwig.

The poor baron bore it all as long as he could, and when he could bear it no longer, lost his appetite and his spirits and sat himself gloomily and dejectedly down. But there were worse troubles yet in store for him, and as they came on, his melancholy and sadness increased. Times changed. He got into debt. The Grogzwig coffers ran low, though the Swillenhausen family had looked upon them as inexhaustible – and just when the baroness was on the point of making a thirteenth addition to the family pedigree, Von Koëldwethout discovered that he had no means of replenishing them.

"I don't see what is to be done," said the baron. "I think I'll kill myself."

This was a bright idea. The baron took an old hunting knife from a cupboard hard by and, having sharpened it on his boot, made what boys call "an offer" at his throat.

"Hem!" said the baron, stopping short. "Perhaps it's not sharp enough."

The baron sharpened it again and made another offer, when his hand was arrested by a loud screaming among the young barons and baronesses, who had a nursery in an upstairs tower, with iron bars outside the windows to prevent their tumbling out into the moat.

"If I had been a bachelor," said the baron, sighing, "I might have done it fifty times over without being interrupted. Hallo! Put a flask of wine and the largest pipe in the little vaulted room behind the hall."

One of the domestics, in a very kind manner, executed the baron's order in the course of half an hour or so, and Von Koëldwethout, being apprised thereof, strode to the vaulted room, the walls of which, being of dark shining wood, gleamed in the light of the blazing logs which were piled upon the hearth. The bottle and pipe were ready and, upon the whole, the place looked very comfortable.

"Leave the lamp," said the baron.

"Anything else, my lord?" enquired the domestic.

"The room," replied the baron. The domestic obeyed, and the baron locked the door.

"I'll smoke a last pipe," said the baron, "and then I'll be off." So, putting the knife upon the table till he wanted it and tossing off a goodly measure of wine, the Lord of Grogzwig threw himself back in his chair, stretched his legs out before the fire and puffed away.

He thought about a great many things – about his present troubles and past days of bachelorship, and about the Lincoln greens, long since dispersed up and down the country, no one knew whither, with the exception of two who had been unfortunately beheaded, and four who had killed themselves with drinking. His mind was running upon bears and boars, when, in the process of draining his glass to the bottom, he raised his eyes and saw, for the first time and with unbounded astonishment, that he was not alone.

No, he was not: for, on the opposite side of the fire, there sat with folded arms a wrinkled hideous figure with deeply sunk and bloodshot eyes, and an immensely long cadaverous face, shadowed by jagged and matted locks of coarse black hair. He wore a kind of tunic of a dull bluish colour – which, the baron observed on regarding it attentively, was clasped or ornamented down the front with coffin handles. His legs, too, were encased in coffin plates as though in armour, and over his left shoulder he wore a short dusky cloak, which seemed made of a remnant of some pall. He took no notice of the baron, but was intently eyeing the fire.

"Halloa!" said the baron, stamping his foot to attract attention.

"Halloa!" replied the stranger, moving his eyes towards the baron, but not his face or himself. "What now?"

"What now!" replied the baron, nothing daunted by his hollow voice and lustreless eyes. "*I* should ask that question. How did you get here?"

"Through the door," replied the figure.

"What are you?" says the baron.

"A man," replied the figure.

"I don't believe it," says the baron.

"Disbelieve it, then," says the figure.

"I will," replied the baron.

The figure looked at the bold Baron of Grogzwig for some time, and then said familiarly:

"There's no coming over you, I see. I am not a man!"

"What are you, then?" asked the baron.

"A genius," replied the figure.

"You don't look much like one," returned the baron scornfully.

"I am the Genius of Despair and Suicide," said the apparition. "Now you know me."

With these words the apparition turned towards the baron, as if composing himself for a talk – and what was very remarkable was that he threw his cloak aside and, displaying a stake, which was run through the centre of his body, pulled it out with a jerk and laid it on the table, as composedly as if it had been a walking stick.

"Now," said the figure, glancing at the hunting knife, "are you ready for me?"

"Not quite," rejoined the baron. "I must finish this pipe first."

"Look sharp, then," said the figure.

"You seem in a hurry," said the baron.

"Why, yes, I am," answered the figure. "They're doing a pretty brisk business in my way over in England and France just now, and my time is a good deal taken up."

"Do you drink?" said the baron, touching the bottle with the bowl of his pipe.

"Nine times out of ten, and then very hard," rejoined the figure drily.

"Never in moderation?" asked the baron.

"Never," replied the figure with a shudder. "That breeds cheerfulness."

The baron took another look at his new friend, whom he thought an uncommonly queer customer, and at length enquired whether he took any active part in such little proceedings as that which he had in contemplation.

"No," replied the figure evasively, "but I am always present."

"Just to see fair, I suppose?" said the baron.

"Just that," replied the figure, playing with his stake and examining the ferrule. "Be as quick as you can, will you? For there's a young gentleman who is afflicted with too much money and leisure wanting me now, I find."

"Going to kill himself because he has too much money!" exclaimed the baron, quite tickled. "Ha! ha! that's a good one." (This was the first time the baron had laughed for many a long day.)

"I say," expostulated the figure, looking very much scared, "don't do that again."

"Why not?" demanded the baron.

"Because it gives me pain all over," replied the figure. "Sigh as much as you please: that does me good."

The baron sighed mechanically at the mention of the word – the figure, brightening up again, handed him the hunting knife with most winning politeness.

"It's not a bad idea, though," said the baron, feeling the edge of the weapon, "a man killing himself because he has too much money."

"Pooh!" said the apparition petulantly. "No better than a man's killing himself because he has none or little."

Whether the genius unintentionally committed himself in saying this, or whether he thought the baron's mind was so thoroughly made up that it didn't matter what he said, I have no means of knowing. I only know that the baron stopped his hand all of a sudden, opened his eyes wide and looked as if quite a new light had come upon him for the first time.

"Why, certainly," said Von Koëldwethout, "nothing is too bad to be retrieved."

"Except empty coffers," cried the genius.

"Well – but they may be one day filled again," said the baron.

"Scolding wives," snarled the genius.

"Oh! They may be made quiet," said the baron.

"Thirteen children," shouted the genius.

"Can't all go wrong, surely," said the baron.

The genius was evidently growing very savage with the baron for holding these opinions all at once, but he tried to laugh it off and said if he would let him know when he had left off joking, he should feel obliged to him.

"But I am not joking: I was never further from it," remonstrated the baron.

"Well, I am glad to hear that," said the genius, looking very grim, "because a joke, without any figure of speech, *is* the death of me. Come! Quit this dreary world at once."

"I don't know," said the baron, playing with the knife. "It's a dreary one certainly, but I don't think yours is much better, for you have not the appearance of being particularly comfortable. That puts me in mind – what security have I that I shall be any the better for going out of the world after all?" he cried, starting up. "I never thought of that."

"Dispatch!" cried the figure, gnashing his teeth.

"Keep off!" said the baron. "I'll brood over miseries no longer, but put a good face on the matter and try the fresh air and the bears again – and if that don't do, I'll talk to the baroness soundly and cut the Von Swillenhausens dead." With this, the baron fell into his chair and laughed so loud and boisterously that the room rang with it.

The figure fell back a pace or two, regarding the baron meanwhile with a look of intense terror, and when he had ceased, caught up the stake, plunged it violently into his body, uttered a frightful howl and disappeared.

Von Koëldwethout never saw it again. Having once made up his mind to action, he soon brought the baroness and the Von Swillenhausens to reason, and died many years afterwards – not a rich man that I am aware of, but certainly a happy one, leaving behind him a numerous family who had been carefully educated in bear- and boar-hunting under his own personal eye. And my advice to all men is that if ever they become hipped and melancholy from similar causes (as very many men do), they look at both sides of the question, applying a magnifying glass to the best one – and if they still feel tempted to retire without leave, that they smoke a large pipe and drink a full bottle first, and profit by the laudable example of the Baron of Grogzwig.

A Confession Found in a Prison
in the Time of Charles II*

I HELD A LIEUTENANT'S COMMISSION in His Majesty's army and served abroad in the campaigns of 1677 and 1678. The treaty of Nijmegen* being concluded, I returned home and, retiring from the service, withdrew to a small estate lying a few miles east of London, which I had recently acquired in right of my wife.

This is the last night I have to live, and I will set down the naked truth without disguise. I was never a brave man, and had always been from my childhood of a secret, sullen, distrustful nature. I speak of myself as if I had passed from the world, for while I write this my grave is digging and my name is written in the black book of death.

Soon after my return to England, my only brother was seized with mortal illness. This circumstance gave me slight or no pain, for since we had been men we had associated but very little together. He was open-hearted and generous, handsomer than I, more accomplished and generally beloved. Those who sought my acquaintance abroad or at home because they were friends of his seldom attached themselves to me long, and would usually say in our first conversation that they were surprised to find two brothers so unlike in their manners and appearance. It was my habit to lead them on to this avowal, for I knew what comparisons they must draw between us, and having a rankling envy in my heart, I sought to justify it to myself.

We had married two sisters. This additional tie between us, as it may appear to some, only estranged us the more. His wife knew me well. I never struggled with any secret jealousy or gall when she was present, but that woman knew it as well as I did. I never raised my eyes at such times but I found hers fixed upon me – I never bent them on the ground or looked another way but I felt that she overlooked me always. It was an inexpressible relief to me when we quarrelled, and a greater relief still when I heard abroad that she was dead. It seems to me now as if some strange and terrible foreshadowing of what has happened since must have hung over us then. I was afraid of her, she haunted me: her fixed and steady look comes back upon me now like the memory of a dark dream and makes my blood run cold.

She died shortly after giving birth to a child – a boy. When my brother knew that all hope of his own recovery was past, he called my wife to his bedside and confided this orphan, a child of four years old, to her protection. He bequeathed to him all the property he had and willed that, in case of the child's death, it should pass to my wife as the only acknowledgement he could make her for her care and love. He exchanged a few brotherly words with me, deploring our long separation, and being exhausted, fell into a slumber from which he never awoke.

We had no children, and as there had been a strong affection between the sisters and my wife had almost supplied the place of a mother to this boy, she loved him as if he had been her own. The child was ardently attached to her, but he was his mother's image in face and spirit, and always mistrusted me.

I can scarcely fix the date when the feeling first came upon me, but I soon began to be uneasy when this child was by. I never roused myself from some moody train of thought but I marked him looking at me – not with mere childish wonder, but with something of the purpose and meaning that I had so often noted in his mother. It was no effort of my fancy, founded on close resemblance of feature and expression. I never could look the boy down. He feared me, but seemed by some instinct to despise me while he did so; and even when he drew back beneath my gaze – as he would when we were alone, to get nearer to the door – he would keep his bright eyes upon me still.

Perhaps I hide the truth from myself, but I do not think that when this began I meditated to do him any wrong. I may have thought how serviceable his inheritance would be to us, and may have wished him dead, but I believe I had no thought of compassing his death. Neither did the idea come upon me at once, but by very slow degrees, presenting itself at first in dim shapes at a very great distance, as men may think of an earthquake or the last day, then drawing nearer and nearer and losing something of its horror and improbability, then coming to be part and parcel – nay, nearly the whole sum and substance – of my daily thoughts, and resolving itself into a question of means and safety, not of doing or abstaining from the deed.

While this was going on within me, I never could bear that the child should see me looking at him, and yet I was under a fascination which made it a kind of business with me to contemplate his slight and fragile figure and think how easily it might be done. Sometimes I would steal upstairs and watch him as he slept, but usually I hovered in the garden near the window of the room in which he learnt his little tasks, and there, as he sat upon a low seat beside my wife, I would peer at him for hours together from behind a tree, starting like the guilty wretch I was at every rustling of a leaf, and still gliding back to look and start again.

Hard by our cottage, but quite out of sight and (if there were any wind astir) of hearing too, was a deep sheet of water. I spent days in shaping with my pocket knife a rough model of a boat, which I finished at last and dropped in the child's way. Then I withdrew to a secret place which he must pass if he stole away alone to swim this bauble and lurked there for his coming. He came neither that day nor the next, though I waited from noon till nightfall. I was sure that I had him in my net, for I had heard him prattling of the toy, and knew that in his infant pleasure he kept it by his side in bed. I felt no weariness or fatigue, but waited patiently, and on the third day he passed me, running joyously along, with his silken hair streaming in the wind and he singing – God have mercy upon me! – singing a merry ballad – who could hardly lisp the words.

I stole down after him, creeping under certain shrubs which grow in that place, and none but devils know with what terror I, a full-grown man, tracked the footsteps of that baby as he approached the water's brink. I was close upon him, had sunk upon my knee and raised my hand to thrust him in, when he saw my shadow in the stream and turned him round.

His mother's ghost was looking from his eyes. The sun burst forth from behind a cloud: it shone in the bright sky, the glistening earth, the clear water, the sparkling drops of rain upon the leaves. There were eyes in everything. The whole great universe of light was there to see the murder done. I know not what he said: he came of bold and manly blood, and child as he was, he did not crouch or fawn upon me. I heard him cry that he would try to love me – not that he did – and then I saw him running back towards the house. The next I saw was my own sword naked in my hand and he lying at my feet stark dead – dabbled here and there with blood but otherwise no different from what I had seen him in his sleep – in the same attitude too, with his cheek resting upon his little hand.

I took him in my arms and laid him – very gently now that he was dead – in a thicket. My wife was from home that day and would not return until the next. Our bedroom window, the only sleeping room on that side of the house, was but a few feet from the ground, and I resolved to descend from it at night and bury him in the garden. I had no thought that I had failed in my design, no thought that the water would be dragged and nothing found, that the money must now lie waste since I must encourage the idea that the child was lost or stolen. All my thoughts were bound up and knotted together in the one absorbing necessity of hiding what I had done.

How I felt when they came to tell me that the child was missing, when I ordered scouts in all directions, when I gasped and trembled at everyone's approach, no tongue can tell or mind of man conceive. I buried him that night. When I parted the boughs and looked into the dark thicket, there was a glow-worm shining like the visible spirit of God upon the murdered child. I glanced down into his grave when I had placed him there and still it gleamed upon his breast: an eye of fire looking up to heaven in supplication to the stars that watched me at my work.

I had to meet my wife and break the news, and give her hope that the child would soon be found. All this I did – with some appearance, I suppose, of being sincere, for I was the object of no suspicion. This done, I sat at the bedroom window all day long and watched the spot where the dreadful secret lay.

It was in a piece of ground which had been dug up to be newly turfed, and which I had chosen on that account as the traces of my spade were less likely to attract attention. The men who laid down the grass must have thought me mad. I called to them continually to expedite their work, ran out and worked beside them, trod down the turf with my feet and hurried them with frantic eagerness. They had finished their task before night, and then I thought myself comparatively safe.

I slept – not as men do who wake refreshed and cheerful, but I did sleep, passing from vague and shadowy dreams of being hunted down to visions of the plot of grass, through which now a hand, and now a foot, and now the head itself was starting out. At this point I always woke and stole to the window to make sure that it was not really so. That done I crept to bed again, and thus I spent the night in fits and starts, getting up and lying down full twenty times, and dreaming the same dream over and over again – which was far worse than lying awake, for every dream had a whole night's suffering of its own. Once I thought the child was alive and that I had never tried to kill him. To wake from that dream was the most dreadful agony of all.

The next day I sat at the window again, never once taking my eyes from the place, which, although it was covered by the grass, was as plain to me – its shape, its size, its depth, its jagged sides and all – as if it had been open to the light of day. When a servant walked across it, I felt as if he must sink in; when he had passed, I looked to see that his feet had not worn the edges. If a bird lighted there, I was in terror lest by some tremendous interposition it should be instrumental in the discovery; if a breath of air sighed across it, to me it whispered murder. There was not a sight or sound – how ordinary, mean or unimportant soever – but was fraught with fear. And in this state of ceaseless watching I spent three days.

On the fourth, there came to the gate one who had served with me abroad, accompanied by a brother officer of his whom I had never seen. I felt that I could not bear to be out of sight of the place.

It was a summer evening, and I bade my people take a table and a flask of wine into the garden. Then I sat down *with my chair upon the grave*, and being assured that nobody could disturb it now, without my knowledge, tried to drink and talk.

They hoped that my wife was well – that she was not obliged to keep her chamber – that they had not frightened her away. What could I do but tell them with a faltering tongue about the child? The officer whom I did not know was a down-looking man and kept his eyes upon the ground while I was speaking. Even that terrified me! I could not divest myself of the idea that he saw something there which caused him to suspect the truth. I asked him hurriedly if he supposed that – and stopped. "That the child has been murdered?" said he, looking mildly at me. "Oh, no! what could a man gain by murdering a poor child?" *I* could have told him what a man gained by such a deed, no one better, but I held my peace and shivered as with an ague.

Mistaking my emotion, they were endeavouring to cheer me with the hope that the boy would certainly be found – great cheer that was for me! – when we heard a low deep howl, and presently there sprung over the wall two great dogs, who, bounding into the garden, repeated the baying sound we had heard before.

"Bloodhounds!" cried my visitors.

What need to tell me that! I had never seen one of that kind in all my life, but I knew what they were and for what purpose they had come. I grasped the elbows of my chair, and neither spoke nor moved.

"They are of the genuine breed," said the man whom I had known abroad, "and being out of exercise have no doubt escaped from their keeper."

Both he and his friend turned to look at the dogs, who with their noses to the ground moved restlessly about, running to and fro, and up and down, and across, and round in circles, careering about like wild things, and all this time taking no notice of us, but ever and again repeating the yell we had heard already, then dropping their noses to the ground again and tracking earnestly here and there. They now began to snuff the earth more eagerly than they had done yet, and although they were still very restless, no longer beat about in such wide circuits, but kept near to one spot and constantly diminished the distance between themselves and me.

At last they came up close to the great chair on which I sat and, raising their frightful howl once more, tried to tear away the wooden rails that kept them from the ground beneath. I saw how I looked in the faces of the two who were with me.

"They scent some prey," said they, both together.

"They scent no prey!" cried I.

"In Heaven's name, move!" said the one I knew, very earnestly, "or you will be torn to pieces."

"Let them tear me limb from limb, I'll never leave this place!" cried I. "Are dogs to hurry men to shameful deaths? Hew them down, cut them in pieces."

"There is some foul mystery here!" said the officer whom I did not know, drawing his sword. "In King Charles's name, assist me to secure this man."

They both set upon me and forced me away, though I fought and bit and caught at them like a madman. After a struggle, they got me quietly between them, and then – my God! – I saw the angry dogs tearing at the earth and throwing it up into the air like water.

What more have I to tell? That I fell upon my knees, and with chattering teeth confessed the truth and prayed to be forgiven. That I have since denied, and now confess to it again. That I have been tried for the crime, found guilty and sentenced. That I have not the courage to anticipate my doom, or to bear up manfully against it. That I have no compassion, no consolation, no hope, no friend. That my wife has happily lost for the time those faculties which would enable her to know my misery or hers. That I am alone in this stone dungeon with my evil spirit, and that I die tomorrow!

To Be Read at Dusk*

ONE, TWO, THREE, FOUR, FIVE. There were five of them.
Five couriers, sitting on a bench outside the convent on the
summit of the Great St Bernard in Switzerland, looking at the
remote heights stained by the setting sun, as if a mighty quantity
of red wine had been broached upon the mountain top and had
not yet had time to sink into the snow.

This is not my simile. It was made for the occasion by the
stoutest courier, who was a German. None of the others took
any more notice of it than they took of me, sitting on another
bench on the other side of the convent door, smoking my cigar,
like them, and – also like them – looking at the reddened snow
and at the lonely shed hard by, where the bodies of belated travellers, dug out of it, slowly wither away, knowing no corruption
in that cold region.

The wine upon the mountain top soaked in as we looked; the
mountain became white; the sky, a very dark blue; the wind rose;
and the air turned piercing cold. The five couriers buttoned their
rough coats. There being no safer man to imitate in all such proceedings than a courier, I buttoned mine.

The mountain in the sunset had stopped the five couriers in a
conversation. It is a sublime sight, likely to stop conversation. The
mountain being now out of the sunset, they resumed. Not that I
had heard any part of their previous discourse, for indeed I had not
then broken away from the American gentleman, in the travellers'
parlour of the convent, who, sitting with his face to the fire, had
undertaken to realize to me the whole progress of events which had
led to the accumulation by the Honourable Ananias Dodger of
one of the largest acquisitions of dollars ever made in one country.

"My God!" said the Swiss courier, speaking in French, which I do
not hold (as some authors appear to do) to be such an all-sufficient

67

excuse for a naughty word that I have only to write it in that language to make it innocent. "If you talk of ghosts…"

"But I *don't* talk of ghosts," said the German.

"Of what then?" asked the Swiss.

"If I knew of what then," said the German, "I should probably know a great deal more."

It was a good answer, I thought, and it made me curious. So I moved my position to that corner of my bench which was nearest to them and, leaning my back against the convent wall, heard perfectly, without appearing to attend.

"Thunder and lightning!" said the German, warming. "When a certain man is coming to see you unexpectedly, and without his own knowledge sends some invisible messenger to put the idea of him into your head all day, what do you call that? When you walk along a crowded street – at Frankfurt, Milan, London, Paris – and think that a passing stranger is like your friend Heinrich, and then that another passing stranger is like your friend Heinrich, and so begin to have a strange foreknowledge that presently you'll meet your friend Heinrich – which you do, though you believed him at Trieste – what do you call *that*?"

"It's not uncommon, either," murmured the Swiss and the other three.

"Uncommon!" said the German. "It's as common as cherries in the Black Forest. It's as common as macaroni at Naples. And Naples reminds me!… When the old Marchesa Senzanima shrieks at a card party on the Chiaia* – as I heard and saw her, for it happened in a Bavarian family of mine, and I was overlooking the service that evening – I say, when the old Marchesa starts up at the card table, white through her rouge, and cries, 'My sister in Spain is dead! I felt her cold touch on my back!' – and when that sister *is* dead at the moment – what do you call that?"

"Or when the blood of San Gennaro liquefies at the request of the clergy – as all the world knows that it does regularly once a year in my native city," said the Neapolitan courier after a pause, with a comical look, "what do you call that?"

"*That*!" cried the German. "Well, I think I know a name for that."

"Miracle?" said the Neapolitan, with the same sly face.

The German merely smoked and laughed – and they all smoked and laughed.

"Bah!" said the German, presently. "I speak of things that really do happen. When I want to see the conjurer, I pay to see a professional one, and have my money's worth. Very strange things do happen without ghosts. Ghosts! Giovanni Battista, tell your story of the English bride. There's no ghost in that, but something full as strange. Will any man tell me what?"

As there was a silence among them, I glanced around. He whom I took to be Battista was lighting a fresh cigar. He presently went on to speak. He was a Genoese, as I judged.

"The story of the English bride?" said he. "Basta! One ought not to call so slight a thing a story. Well, it's all one. But it's true. Observe me well, gentlemen, it's true. That which glitters is not always gold – but what I am going to tell is true."

He repeated this more than once.

"Ten years ago, I took my credentials to an English gentleman at Long's Hotel, in Bond Street, London, who was about to travel – it might be for one year, it might be for two. He approved of them – likewise of me. He was pleased to make enquiry. The testimony that he received was favourable. He engaged me by the six months, and my entertainment was generous.

"He was young, handsome, very happy. He was enamoured of a fair young English lady, with a sufficient fortune, and they were going to be married. It was the wedding trip, in short, that we were going to take. For three months' rest in the hot weather (it was early summer then) he had hired an old place on the Riviera, at an easy distance from my city, Genoa, on the road to Nice. Did I know that place? Yes – I told him I knew it well. It was an old palace with great gardens. It was a little bare, and it was a little dark and gloomy, being close-surrounded by trees, but it was spacious, ancient, grand and on the seashore. He said it had been so described to him exactly, and he was well pleased that I knew it. For its being a little bare of furniture, all such places were. For its being a little gloomy, he had hired it principally for the gardens, and he and my mistress would pass the summer weather in their shade.

"'So all goes well, Battista?' said he.

"'Indubitably, signore, very well.'

"We had a travelling chariot for our journey, newly built for us, and in all respects complete. All we had was complete: we wanted for nothing. The marriage took place. They were happy. *I* was happy, seeing all was bright, being so well situated, going to my own city, teaching my language in the rumble to the maid, *la bella* Carolina, whose heart was gay with laughter – who was young and rosy.

"The time flew. But I observed – listen to this, I pray!" – and here the courier dropped his voice – "I observed my mistress sometimes brooding in a manner very strange – in a frightened manner – in an unhappy manner – with a cloudy, uncertain alarm upon her. I think that I began to notice this when I was walking up hills by the carriage side, and master had gone on in front. At any rate, I remember that it impressed itself upon my mind one evening in the South of France, when she called to me to call master back, and when he came back and walked for a long way talking encouragingly and affectionately to her, with his hand upon the open window and hers in it. Now and then, he laughed in a merry way, as if he were bantering her out of something. By and by, she laughed, and then all went well again.

"It was curious. I asked *la bella* Carolina, the pretty little one, was mistress unwell? – No. – Out of spirits? – No. – Fearful of bad roads or brigands? – No. And what made it more mysterious was the pretty little one would not look at me in giving answer, but *would* look at the view.

"But one day she told me the secret.

"'If you must know,' said Carolina, 'I find, from what I have overheard, that mistress is haunted.'

"'How haunted?'

"'By a dream.'

"'What dream?'

"'By a dream of a face. For three nights before her marriage, she saw a face in a dream – always the same face, and only one.'

"'A terrible face?'

"'No. The face of a dark, remarkable-looking man, in black, with black hair and a grey moustache – a handsome man except for a reserved and secret air. Not a face she ever saw, or at all like a face she ever saw. Doing nothing in the dream but looking at her fixedly, out of darkness.'

"'Does the dream come back?'

"'Never. The recollection of it is all her trouble.'

"'And why does it trouble her?'

"Carolina shook her head.

"'That's master's question,' said *la bella*. 'She don't know. She wonders why herself. But I heard her tell him, only last night, that if she was to find a picture of that face in our Italian house (which she is afraid she will), she did not know how she could ever bear it.'

"Upon my word, I was fearful after this" – said the Genoese courier – "of our coming to the old palazzo, lest some such ill-starred picture should happen to be there. I knew there were many there, and as we got nearer and nearer to the place, I wished the whole gallery in the crater of Vesuvius. To mend the matter, it was a stormy dismal evening when we, at last, approached that part of the Riviera. It thundered, and the thunder of my city and its environs, rolling among the high hills, is very loud. The lizards ran in and out of the chinks in the broken stone wall of the garden, as if they were frightened; the frogs bubbled and croaked their loudest; the sea wind moaned, and the wet trees dripped; and the lightning – body of San Lorenzo, how it lightened!

"We all know what an old palace in or near Genoa is – how time and the sea air have blotted it – how the drapery painted on the outer walls has peeled off in great flakes of plaster – how the lower windows are darkened with rusty bars of iron – how the courtyard is overgrown with grass – how the outer buildings are dilapidated – how the whole pile seems devoted to ruin. Our palazzo was one of the true kind. It has been shut up close for months. Months? – years! – it had an earthy smell, like a tomb. The scent of the orange trees on the broad back terrace, and of the lemons ripening on the wall, and of some shrubs that grew around a broken fountain, had got into the house somehow and had never been able to get out again. There was, in every room, an aged smell, grown faint with confinement. It pined in all the cupboards and drawers. In the little rooms of communication between great rooms, it was stifling. If you turned a picture – to come back to the pictures – there it still was, clinging to the wall behind the frame, like a sort of bat.

"The lattice blinds were close shut, all over the house. There were two ugly grey old women in the house to take care of it: one of them with a spindle, who stood winding and mumbling in the doorway and who would as soon have let in the Devil as the air. Master, mistress, *la bella* Carolina and I went all through the palazzo. I went first, though I have named myself last, opening the windows and the lattice blinds and shaking down on myself splashes of rain and scraps of mortar, and now and then a dozing mosquito or a monstrous, fat, blotchy Genoese spider.

"When I had let the evening light into a room, master, mistress and *la bella* Carolina entered. Then we looked round at all the pictures, and I went forward again into another room. Mistress secretly had great fear of meeting with the likeness of that face – we all had – but there was no such thing. The Madonna and Bambino, San Francesco, San Sebastiano, Venus, Santa Caterina, Angels, Brigands, Friars, Temples at Sunset, Battles, White Horses, Forests, Apostles, Doges, all my old acquaintances many times repeated? – yes. Dark handsome man in black, reserved and secret, with black hair and grey moustache, looking fixedly at mistress out of darkness? – no.

"At last we got through all the rooms and all the pictures and came out into the gardens. They were pretty well kept, being rented by a gardener, and were large and shady. In one place there was a rustic theatre, open to the sky; the stage a green slope; the coulisses, three entrances upon a side, sweet-smelling leafy screens. Mistress moved her bright eyes, even there, as if she looked to see the face come in upon the scene – but all was well.

"'Now, Clara,' master said, in a low voice, 'you see that it is nothing? You are happy.'

"Mistress was much encouraged. She soon accustomed herself to that grim palazzo, and would sing and play the harp, and copy the old pictures, and stroll with master under the green trees and vines all day. She was beautiful. He was happy. He would laugh and say to me, mounting his horse for his morning ride before the heat:

"'All goes well, Battista!'

"'Yes, signore, thank God, very well.'

"We kept no company. I took *la bella* to the Duomo and Annunziata, to the café, to the opera, to the village festa, to the public garden, to the day theatre, to the marionette.* The pretty little one was charmed with all she saw. She learnt Italian – heavens! miraculously! Was mistress quite forgetful of that dream? I asked Carolina sometimes. Nearly, said *la bella* – almost. It was wearing out.

"One day master received a letter and called me.

"'Battista!'

"'Signore!'

"'A gentleman who is presented to me will dine here today. He is called the Signor Dellombra. Let me dine like a prince.'

"It was an odd name.* I did not know that name. But there had been many noblemen and gentlemen pursued by Austria on political suspicions, lately, and some names had changed. Perhaps this was one. Altro!* Dellombra was as good a name to me as another.

"When the Signor Dellombra came to dinner" – said the Genoese courier in the low voice into which he had subsided once before – "I showed him into the reception room, the great sala of the old palazzo. Master received him with cordiality and presented him to mistress. As she rose, her face changed: she gave a cry and fell upon the marble floor.

"Then I turned my head to the Signor Dellombra and saw that he was dressed in black and had a reserved and secret air, and was a dark, remarkable-looking man, with black hair and a grey moustache.

"Master raised mistress in his arms and carried her to her own room, where I sent *la bella* Carolina straight. *La bella* told me afterwards that mistress was nearly terrified to death, and that she wandered in her mind about her dream all night.

73

"Master was vexed and anxious – almost angry, and yet full of solicitude. The Signor Dellombra was a courtly gentleman, and spoke with great respect and sympathy of mistress's being so ill. The African wind had been blowing for some days (they had told him at his hotel of the Maltese Cross), and he knew that it was often hurtful. He hoped the beautiful lady would recover soon. He begged permission to retire and to renew his visit when he should have the happiness of hearing that she was better. Master would not allow of this, and they dined alone.

"He withdrew early. Next day he called at the gate, on horse-back, to enquire for mistress. He did so two or three times in that week.

"What I observed myself, and what *la bella* Carolina told me, united to explain to me that master had now set his mind on curing mistress of her fanciful terror. He was all kindness, but he was sensible and firm. He reasoned with her that to encourage such fancies was to invite melancholy, if not madness. That it rested with herself to be herself. That if she once resisted her strange weakness, so successfully as to receive the Signor Dellombra as an English lady would receive any other guest, it was for ever conquered. To make an end, the signore came again, and mistress received him without marked distress (though with constraint and apprehension still), and the evening passed serenely. Master was so delighted with this change, and so anxious to confirm it, that the Signor Dellombra became a constant guest. He was accomplished in pictures, books and music, and his society, in any grim palazzo, would have been welcome.

"I used to notice, many times, that mistress was not quite recov-ered. She would cast down her eyes and droop her head before the Signor Dellombra, or would look at him with a terrified and fas-cinated glance, as if his presence had some evil influence or power upon her. Turning from her to him, I used to see him in the shaded gardens or the large half-lighted sala looking, as I might say, 'fixedly upon her out of darkness'. But, truly, I had not forgotten *la bella* Carolina's words describing the face in the dream.

"After his second visit I heard master say:

"'Now, see, my dear Clara, it's over! Dellombra has come and gone, and your apprehension is broken like glass.'

"'Will he – will he ever come again?' asked mistress.

"'Again? Why, surely, over and over again! Are you cold?' (She shivered.)

"'No, dear – but he terrifies me: are you sure that he need come again?'

"'The surer for the question, Clara!' replied master, cheerfully.

"But he was very hopeful of her complete recovery now, and grew more and more so every day. She was beautiful. He was happy.

"'All goes well, Battista?' he would say to me again.

"'Yes, signore, thank God – very well.'

"We were all" – said the Genoese courier, constraining himself to speak a little louder – "we were all at Rome for the Carnival. I had been out, all day, with a Sicilian, a friend of mine, and a courier, who was there with an English family. As I returned at night to our hotel, I met the little Carolina, who never stirred from home alone, running distractedly along the Corso.

"'Carolina! What's the matter?'

"'Oh Battista! Oh, for the Lord's sake! where is my mistress?'

"'Mistress, Carolina?'

"'Gone since morning – told me, when master went out on his day's journey, not to call her, for she was tired with not resting in the night (having been in pain) and would lie in bed until the evening, then get up refreshed. She is gone! – she is gone! Master has come back, broken down the door, and she is gone! My beautiful, my good, my innocent mistress!'

"The pretty little one so cried and raved and tore herself that I could not have held her but for her swooning on my arm as if she had been shot. Master came up – in manner, face or voice no more the master that I knew than I was he. He took me (I laid the little one upon her bed in the hotel and left her with the chamberwoman) in a carriage, furiously through the darkness, across the desolate Campagna. When it was day and we stopped at a miserable post house, all the horses had been hired twelve hours ago and sent away in different directions – sent away, mark me! by the Signor

Dellombra, who had passed there in a carriage, with a frightened English lady crouching in one corner.

"I never heard" – said the Genoese courier, drawing a long breath – "that she was ever traced beyond that spot. All I know is that she vanished into infamous oblivion with the dreaded face beside her that she had seen in her dream."

"What do you call *that*?" said the German courier, triumphantly. "Ghosts! There are no ghosts *there*! What do you call this that I am going to tell you? Ghosts! There are no ghosts *here*! I took an engagement once" – pursued the German courier – "with an English gentleman, elderly and a bachelor, to travel through my country, my Fatherland. He was a merchant who traded with my country and knew the language, but who had never been there since he was a boy – as I judge, some sixty years before.

"His name was James, and he had a twin brother, John, also a bachelor. Between these brothers there was a great affection. They were in business together, at Goodman's Fields, but they did not live together. Mr James dwelt in Poland Street, turning out of Oxford Street, London; Mr John resided by Epping Forest.

"Mr James and I were to start for Germany in about a week. The exact day depended on business. Mr John came to Poland Street (where I was staying in the house) to pass that week with Mr James. But he said to his brother on the second day, 'I don't feel very well, James. There's not much the matter with me, but I think I am a little gouty. I'll go home and put myself under the care of my old housekeeper, who understands my ways. If I get quite better, I'll come back and see you before you go. If I don't feel well enough to resume my visit where I leave it off, why *you* will come and see *me* before you go.' Mr James, of course, said he would, and they shook hands – both hands, as they always did – and Mr John ordered out his old-fashioned chariot and rumbled home.

"It was on the second night after that – that is to say, the fourth in the week – when I was awoke out of my sound sleep by Mr James coming into my bedroom in his flannel gown, with a lighted candle. He sat upon the side of my bed and, looking at me, said:

"'Wilhelm, I have reason to think I have got some strange illness upon me.'

"I then perceived that there was a very unusual expression in his face.

"'Wilhelm,' said he, 'I am not afraid or ashamed to tell you what I might be afraid or ashamed to tell another man. You come from a sensible country, where mysterious things are inquired into and are not settled to have been weighed and measured – or to have been unweighable and unmeasurable – or in either case to have been completely disposed of, for all time – ever so many years ago. I have just now seen the phantom of my brother.'

"I confess" – said the German courier – "that it gave me a little tingling of the blood to hear it.

"'I have just now seen,' Mr James repeated, looking full at me, that I might see how collected he was, 'the phantom of my brother John. I was sitting up in bed, unable to sleep, when it came into my room, in a white dress, and regarding me earnestly, passed up to the end of the room, glanced at some papers on my writing desk, turned and, still looking earnestly at me as it passed the bed, went out at the door. Now, I am not in the least mad, and am not in the least disposed to invest that phantom with any external existence out of myself. I think it is a warning to me that I am ill – and I think I had better be bled.'

"I got out of bed directly" – said the German courier – "and began to get on my clothes, begging him not to be alarmed, and telling him that I would go myself to the doctor. I was just ready, when we heard a loud knocking and ringing at the street door. My room being an attic at the back, and Mr James's being the second-floor room in the front, we went down to his room and put up the window, to see what was the matter.

"'Is that Mr James?' said a man below, falling back to the opposite side of the way to look up.

"'It is,' said Mr James, 'and you are my brother's man, Robert.'

"'Yes, sir. I am sorry to say, sir, that Mr John is ill. He is very bad, sir. It is even feared that he may be lying at the point of death. He wants to see you, sir. I have a chaise here. Pray come to him. Pray lose no time.'

"Mr James and I looked at one another. 'Wilhelm,' said he, 'this is strange. I wish you to come with me!' I helped him to dress, partly there and partly in the chaise – and no grass grew under the horses' iron shoes between Poland Street and the Forest.

"Now, mind!" – said the German courier – "I went with Mr James into his brother's room, and I saw and heard myself what follows.

"His brother lay upon his bed, at the upper end of a long bed-chamber. His old housekeeper was there, and others were there – I think three others were there, if not four, and they had been with him since early in the afternoon. He was in white, like the figure – necessarily so, because he had his nightdress on. He looked like the figure – necessarily so, because he looked earnestly at his brother when he saw him come into the room.

"But when his brother reached the bedside, he slowly raised himself in bed and, looking full upon him, said these words:

"'*James, you have seen me before tonight – and you know it!*'

"And so he died."

I waited, when the German courier ceased, to hear something said of this strange story. The silence was unbroken. I looked round, and the five couriers were gone – so noiselessly that the ghostly mountain might have absorbed them into its eternal snows. By this time, I was by no means in a mood to sit alone in that awful scene, with the chill air coming solemnly upon me – or, if I may tell the truth, to sit alone anywhere. So I went back into the convent parlour, and finding the American gentleman still disposed to relate the biography of the Honourable Ananias Dodger, heard it all out.

The Ghost in the Bride's Chamber*

T HE HOUSE was a genuine old house of a very quaint description, teeming with old carvings and beams and panels, and
having an excellent old staircase, with a gallery or upper staircase
cut off from it by a curious fence work of old oak, or of the old
Honduras mahogany wood. It was and is, and will be for many a
long year to come, a remarkably picturesque house, and a certain
grave mystery lurking in the depth of the old mahogany panels, as
if they were so many deep pools of dark water – such, indeed, as
they had been much among when they were trees – gave it a very
mysterious character after nightfall.

When Mr Goodchild and Mr Idle had first alighted at the door
and stepped into the sombre, handsome old hall, they had been
received by half a dozen noiseless old men in black, all dressed
exactly alike, who glided up the stairs with the obliging landlord
and waiter – but without appearing to get into their way or to mind
whether they did or no – and who had filed off to the right and left
on the old staircase as the guests entered their sitting room. It was
then broad, bright day. But Mr Goodchild had said, when their
door was shut, "Who on earth are these old men?" And afterwards,
both on going out and coming in, he had noticed that there were
no old men to be seen.

Neither had the old men, or any one of the old men, reappeared
since. The two friends had passed a night in the house, but had seen
nothing more of the old men. Mr Goodchild, in rambling about
it, had looked along passages and glanced in at doorways, but had
encountered no old men – neither did it appear that any old men
were, by any member of the establishment, missed or expected.

Another odd circumstance impressed itself on their attention. It
was that the door of their sitting room was never left untouched
for a quarter of an hour. It was opened with hesitation, opened

with confidence, opened a little way, opened a good way – always clapped-to again without a word of explanation. They were reading, they were writing, they were eating, they were drinking, they were talking, they were dozing – the door was always opened at an unexpected moment, and they looked towards it and it was clapped-to again, and nobody was to be seen. When this had happened fifty times or so, Mr Goodchild had said to his companion, jestingly: "I begin to think, Tom, there was something wrong with those six old men."

Night had come again, and they had been writing for two or three hours: writing, in short, a portion of the lazy notes from which these lazy sheets are taken. They had left off writing, and glasses were on the table between them. The house was closed and quiet. Around the head of Thomas Idle, as he lay upon his sofa, hovered light wreaths of fragrant smoke. The temples of Francis Goodchild, as he leaned back in his chair with his two hands clasped behind his head and his legs crossed, were similarly decorated.

They had been discussing several idle subjects of speculation, not omitting the strange old men, and were still so occupied when Mr Goodchild abruptly changed his attitude to wind up his watch. They were just becoming drowsy enough to be stopped in their talk by any such slight check. Thomas Idle, who was speaking at the moment, paused and said, "How goes it?"

"One," said Goodchild.

As if he had ordered One old man and the order were promptly executed (truly, all orders were so in that excellent hotel), the door opened and One old man stood there.

He did not come in, but stood with the door in his hand.

"One of the six, Tom, at last!" said Mr Goodchild, in a surprised whisper. "Sir, your pleasure?"

"Sir, *your* pleasure?" said the One old man.

"I didn't ring."

"The bell did," said the One old man.

He said "bell" in a deep, strong way that would have expressed the church bell.

"I had the pleasure, I believe, of seeing you yesterday?" said Goodchild.

"I cannot undertake to say for certain," was the grim reply of the One old man.

"I think you saw me? Did you not?"

"Saw *you*?" said the old man. "Oh yes, I saw *you*. But I see many who never see me."

A chilled, slow, earthy, fixed old man. A cadaverous old man of measured speech. An old man who seemed as unable to wink as if his eyelids had been nailed to his forehead. An old man whose eyes – two spots of fire – had no more motion than if they had been connected with the back of his skull by screws driven through it and riveted and bolted outside, among his grey hairs.

The night had turned so cold, to Mr Goodchild's sensations, that he shivered. He remarked lightly, and half apologetically: "I think somebody is walking over my grave."

"No," said the weird old man, "there is no one there."

Mr Goodchild looked at Idle, but Idle lay with his head enwreathed in smoke.

"No one there?" said Goodchild.

"There is no one at your grave, I assure you," said the old man.

He had come in and shut the door, and he now sat down. He did not bend himself to sit, as other people do, but seemed to sink bolt-upright, as if in water, until the chair stopped him.

"My friend, Mr Idle," said Goodchild, extremely anxious to introduce a third person into the conversation.

"I am," said the old man, without looking at him, "at Mr Idle's service."

"If you are an old inhabitant of this place..." Francis Goodchild resumed.

"Yes."

"...Perhaps you can decide a point my friend and I were in doubt upon, this morning. They hang condemned criminals at the Castle, I believe?"

"*I* believe so," said the old man.

"Are their faces turned towards that noble prospect?"

"Your face is turned," replied the old man, "to the Castle wall. When you are tied up, you see its stones expanding and contracting violently, and a similar expansion and contraction seem to take place in your own head and breast. Then, there is a rush of fire and an earthquake, and the Castle springs into the air, and you tumble down a precipice."

His cravat seemed to trouble him. He put his hand to his throat and moved his neck from side to side. He was an old man of a swollen character of face, and his nose was immovably hitched up on one side, as if by a little hook inserted in that nostril. Mr Goodchild felt exceedingly uncomfortable and began to think the night was hot, and not cold.

"A strong description, sir," he observed.

"A strong sensation," the old man rejoined.

Again, Mr Goodchild looked to Mr Thomas Idle, but Thomas lay on his back with his face attentively turned towards the One old man, and made no sign. At this time Mr Goodchild believed that he saw threads of fire stretch from the old man's eyes to his own and there attach themselves. (Mr Goodchild writes the present account of his experience and, with the utmost solemnity, protests that he had the strongest sensation upon him of being forced to look at the old man along those two fiery films, from that moment.)

"I must tell it to you," said the old man, with a ghastly and a stony stare.

"What?" asked Francis Goodchild.

"You know where it took place. Yonder!"

Whether he pointed to the room above or to the room below, or to any room in that old house, or to a room in some other old house in that old town, Mr Goodchild was not, nor is, nor ever can be sure. He was confused by the circumstance that the right forefinger of the One old man seemed to dip itself in one of the threads of fire, light itself and make a fiery start in the air as it pointed somewhere. Having pointed somewhere, it went out.

"You know she was a Bride," said the old man.

"I know they still send up Bride cake," Mr Goodchild faltered. "This is a very oppressive air."

"She was a Bride," said the old man. "She was a fair, flaxen-haired, large-eyed girl who had no character, no purpose. A weak, credulous, incapable, helpless nothing. Not like her mother. No, no. It was her father whose character she reflected.

"Her mother had taken care to secure everything to herself, for her own life, when the father of this girl (a child at that time) died – of sheer helplessness, no other disorder – and then He renewed the acquaintance that had once subsisted between the mother and Him. He had been put aside for the flaxen-haired, large-eyed man (or nonentity) with Money. He could overlook that for Money. He wanted compensation in Money.

"So he returned to the side of that woman the mother, made love to her again, danced attendance on her and submitted himself to her whims. She wreaked upon him every whim she had or could invent. He bore it. And the more he bore, the more he wanted compensation in Money, and the more he was resolved to have it.

"But lo! Before he got it, she cheated him. In one of her imperious states, she froze, and never thawed again. She put her hands to her head one night, uttered a cry, stiffened, lay in that attitude certain hours and died. Again he had got no compensation from her in Money, yet. Blight and Murrain on her! Not a penny.

"He had hated her throughout that second pursuit, and had longed for retaliation on her. He now counterfeited her signature to an instrument, leaving all she had to leave to her daughter – ten years old then – to whom the property passed absolutely, and appointed himself the daughter's Guardian. When He slid it under the pillow of the bed on which she lay, He bent down in the deaf ear of Death and whispered: 'Mistress Pride, I have determined a long time that, dead or alive, you must make me compensation in Money.'

"So now there were only two left. Which two were He and the fair, flaxen-haired, large-eyed foolish daughter, who afterwards became the Bride.

"He put her to school. In a secret, dark, oppressive, ancient house, he put her to school with a watchful and unscrupulous woman. 'My worthy lady,' he said, 'here is a mind to be formed – will you help me to form it?' She accepted the trust. For which she, too, wanted compensation in Money, and had it.

"The girl was formed in the fear of him, and in the conviction that there was no escape from him. She was taught, from the first, to regard him as her future husband – the man who must marry her – the destiny that overshadowed her – the appointed certainty that could never be evaded. The poor fool was soft white wax in their hands, and took the impression that they put upon her. It hardened with time. It became a part of herself. Inseparable from herself, and only to be torn away from her by tearing life away from her.

"Eleven years she had lived in the dark house and its gloomy garden. He was jealous of the very light and air getting to her, and they kept her close. He stopped the wide chimneys, shaded the little windows, left the strong-stemmed ivy to wander where it would over the house front, the moss to accumulate on the untrimmed fruit trees in the red-walled garden, the weeds to over-run its green and yellow walks. He surrounded her with images of sorrow and desolation. He caused her to be filled with fears of the place and of the stories that were told of it, and then on pretext of correcting them, to be left in it in solitude, or made to shrink about it in the dark. When her mind was most depressed and fullest of terrors, then he would come out of one of the hiding places from which he overlooked her and present himself as her sole recourse.

"Thus, by being from her childhood the one embodiment her life presented to her of power to coerce and power to relieve, power to bind and power to loose, the ascendency over her weakness was secured. She was twenty-one years and twenty-one days old when he brought her home to the gloomy house, his half-witted, frightened and submissive Bride of three weeks.

"He had dismissed the governess by that time – what he had left to do, he could best do alone – and they came back, upon a rainy night, to the scene of her long preparation. She turned to him upon the threshold, as the rain was dripping from the porch, and said:

"'Oh sir, it is the Death watch ticking for me!'

"'Well!' he answered. 'And if it were?'

"'Oh sir!' she returned to him, 'look kindly on me, and be merciful to me! I beg your pardon. I will do anything you wish, if you will only forgive me!'

"That had become the poor fool's constant song: 'I beg your pardon' and 'Forgive me!'

"She was not worth hating: he felt nothing but contempt for her. But she had long been in the way, and he had long been weary, and the work was near its end and had to be worked out.

"'You fool,' he said. 'Go up the stairs!'

"She obeyed very quickly, murmuring, 'I will do anything you wish!' When he came into the Bride's Chamber, having been a little retarded by the heavy fastenings of the great door (for they were alone in the house, and he had arranged that the people who attended on them should come and go in the day), he found her withdrawn to the farthest corner, and there standing pressed against the panelling as if she would have shrunk through it, her flaxen hair all wild about her face and her large eyes staring at him in vague terror.

"'What are you afraid of? Come and sit down by me.'

"'I will do anything you wish. I beg your pardon, sir. Forgive me!' Her monotonous tune as usual.

"'Ellen, here is a writing that you must write out tomorrow, in your own hand. You may as well be seen by others busily engaged upon it. When you have written it all fairly and corrected all mistakes, call in any two people there may be about the house and sign your name to it before them. Then put it in your bosom to keep it safe, and when I sit here again tomorrow night, give it to me.'

"'I will do it all, with the greatest care. I will do anything you wish.'

"'Don't shake and tremble, then.'

"'I will try my utmost not to do it – if you will only forgive me!'

"Next day, she sat down at her desk and did as she had been told. He often passed in and out of the room to observe her, and always saw her slowly and laboriously writing, repeating to herself the words she copied, in appearance quite mechanically, and without caring or endeavouring to comprehend them, so that she did her task. He saw her follow the directions she had received, in all particulars; and at night, when they were alone again in the same Bride's Chamber and he drew his chair to the hearth, she timidly approached him from her distant seat, took the paper from her bosom and gave it into his hand.

"It secured all her possessions to him in the event of her death. He put her before him face to face, that he might look at her steadily, and he asked her, in so many plain words, neither fewer nor more, did she know that?

"There were spots of ink upon the bosom of her white dress, and they made her face look whiter and her eyes look larger as she nodded her head. There were spots of ink upon the hand with which she stood before him, nervously plaiting and folding her white skirts.

"He took her by the arm and looked her, yet more closely and steadily, in the face. 'Now, die! I have done with you.'

"She shrunk and uttered a low, suppressed cry.

"'I am not going to kill you. I will not endanger my life for yours. Die!'

"He sat before her in the gloomy Bride's Chamber, day after day, night after night, looking the word at her when he did not utter it. As often as her large unmeaning eyes were raised from the hands in which she rocked her head to the stern figure sitting with crossed arms and knitted forehead in the chair, they read in it: 'Die!' When she dropped asleep in exhaustion, she was called back to shuddering consciousness by the whisper 'Die!' When she fell upon her old entreaty to be pardoned, she was answered, 'Die!' When she had out-watched and out-suffered the long night, and the rising sun flamed into the sombre room, she heard it hailed with 'Another day and not dead?... Die!'

"Shut up in the deserted mansion, aloof from all mankind and engaged alone in such a struggle without any respite, it came to this – that either he must die or she. He knew it very well, and concentrated his strength against her feebleness. Hours upon hours he held her by the arm when her arm was black where he held it, and bade her: 'Die!'

"It was done upon a windy morning, before sunrise. He computed the time to be half-past four, but his forgotten watch had run down, and he could not be sure. She had broken away from him in the night, with loud and sudden cries – the first of that kind to which she had given vent – and he had had to put his hands over her mouth. Since then, she had been quiet in the corner of the panelling where she had sunk down; and he had left her, and had gone back with his folded arms and his knitted forehead to his chair.

"Paler in the pale light, more colourless than ever in the leaden dawn, he saw her coming, trailing herself along the floor towards him – a white wreck of hair and dress and wild eyes pushing itself on by an irresolute and bending hand.

"'Oh, forgive me! I will do anything. Oh, sir, pray tell me I may live!'

"'Die!'

"'Are you so resolved? Is there no hope for me?'

"'Die!'

"Her large eyes strained themselves with wonder and fear – wonder and fear changed to reproach – reproach to blank nothing. It was done. He was not at first so sure it was done, but that the morning sun was hanging jewels in her hair – he saw the diamond, emerald and ruby glittering among it in little points as he stood looking down at her – when he lifted her and laid her on her bed.

"She was soon laid in the ground. And now they were all gone, and he had compensated himself well.

"He had a mind to travel. Not that he meant to waste his Money, for he was a pinching man and liked his Money dearly (like nothing else, indeed), but that he had grown tired of the desolate house and wished to turn his back upon it and have done with it. But the house was worth Money, and Money must not be thrown away. He determined to sell it before he went. That it might look the less wretched and bring a better price, he hired some labourers to work in the overgrown garden – to cut out the dead wood, trim the ivy that dropped in heavy masses over the windows and gables, and clear the walks in which the weeds were growing mid-leg high.

"He worked himself along with them. He worked later than they did, and one evening at dusk was left working alone, with his billhook in his hand. One autumn evening, when the Bride was five weeks dead.

"'It grows too dark to work longer,' he said to himself, 'I must give over for the night.'

"He detested the house, and was loath to enter it. He looked at the dark porch waiting for him like a tomb, and felt that it was an accursed house. Near to the porch, and near to where he stood, was a tree whose branches waved before the old bay window of the Bride's Chamber, where it had been done. The tree swung suddenly and made him start. It swung again, although the night was still. Looking up into it, he saw a figure among the branches.

"It was the figure of a young man. The face looked down as he looked up – the branches cracked and swayed – the figure rapidly descended and slid upon its feet before him. A slender youth of about her age, with long, light-brown hair.

"'What thief are you?' he said, seizing the youth by the collar.

"The young man, in shaking himself free, swung him a blow with his arm across the face and throat. They closed, but the young man got from him and stepped back, crying, with great eagerness and horror, 'Don't touch me! I would as lief be touched by the Devil!'

"He stood still, with his billhook in his hand, looking at the young man. For the young man's look was the counterpart of her last look, and he had not expected ever to see that again.

"'I am no thief. Even if I were, I would not have a coin of your wealth, if it would buy me the Indies. You murderer!'

"'What!'

"'I climbed it,' said the young man, pointing up into the tree, 'for the first time nigh four years ago. I climbed it to look at her. I saw her. I spoke to her. I have climbed it many a time to watch and listen for her. I was a boy, hidden among its leaves, when from that bay window she gave me this!'

"He showed a tress of flaxen hair, tied with a mourning ribbon.

"'Her life,' said the young man, 'was a life of mourning. She gave me this as a token of it and a sign that she was dead to everyone but you. If I had been older, if I had seen her sooner, I might have saved her from you. But she was fast in the web when I first climbed the tree, and what could I do then to break it!'

"In saying these words, he burst into a fit of sobbing and crying: weakly at first, then passionately.

"'Murderer! I climbed the tree on the night when you brought her back. I heard her, from the tree, speak of the Death-watch at the door. I was three times in the tree while you were shut up with her, slowly killing her. I saw her, from the tree, lie dead upon her bed. I have watched you, from the tree, for proofs and traces of your guilt. The manner of it is a mystery to me yet, but I will pursue you until you have rendered up your life to the hangman. You shall never, until then, be rid of me. I loved her! I can know no relenting towards you. Murderer, I loved her!'

"The youth was bareheaded, his hat having fluttered away in his descent from the tree. He moved towards the gate. He had to pass... Him to get to it. There was breadth for two old-fashioned carriages abreast, and the youth's abhorrence, openly expressed in every feature of his face and limb of his body, and very hard to bear, had verge enough to keep itself at a distance in. He (by which I mean the other) had not stirred hand or feet, since he had stood still to look at the boy. He faced round, now, to follow him with his eyes. As the back of the bare light-brown head was turned to him, he saw a red curve stretch from his hand to it. He knew, before he threw the billhook, where it had alighted – I say 'had alighted' and not 'would alight', for to his clear perception the thing was done before he did it. It cleft the head and it remained there, and the boy lay on his face.

"He buried the body in the night, at the foot of the tree. As soon as it was light in the morning, he worked at turning up all the ground near the tree and hacking and hewing at the neighbouring bushes and undergrowth. When the labourers came, there was nothing suspicious, and nothing suspected.

"But he had, in a moment, defeated all his precautions and destroyed the triumph of the scheme he had so long concerted and so successfully worked out. He had got rid of the Bride and had acquired her fortune without endangering his life, but now, for a death by which he had gained nothing, he had evermore to live with a rope around his neck.

"Beyond this, he was chained to the house of gloom and horror, which he could not endure. Being afraid to sell it or to quit it, lest discovery should be made, he was forced to live in it. He hired two old people, man and wife, for his servants – and dwelt in it, and dreaded it. His great difficulty, for a long time, was the garden. Whether he should keep it trim, whether he should suffer it to fall into its former state of neglect – what would be the least likely way of attracting attention to it?

"He took the middle course of gardening himself in his evening leisure and of then calling the old servingman to help him, but of never letting him work there alone. And he made himself an arbour over against the tree, where he could sit and see that it was safe.

"As the seasons changed and the tree changed, his mind perceived dangers that were always changing. In the leafy time, he perceived that the upper boughs were growing into the form of the young man – that they made the shape of him exactly, sitting in a forked branch swinging in the wind. In the time of the falling leaves, he perceived that they came down from the tree, forming telltale letters on the path, or that they had a tendency to heap themselves into a churchyard mound above the grave. In the winter, when the tree was bare, he perceived that the boughs swung at him the ghost of the blow the young man had given, and that they threatened him openly. In the spring, when sap was mounting in the trunk, he asked himself: were the dried-up particles of blood mounting with it – to make out more obviously this year than last the leaf-screened figure of the young man swinging in the wind?

"However, he turned his Money over and over, and still over. He was in the dark trade, the gold-dust trade, and most secret trades that yielded great returns. In ten years, he had turned his Money over so many times that the traders and shippers who had dealings with him absolutely did not lie – for once – when they declared that he had increased his fortune Twelve Hundred Per Cent.

"He possessed his riches one hundred years ago, when people could be lost easily. He had heard who the youth was from hearing of the search that was made after him, but it died away, and the youth was forgotten.

"The annual round of changes in the tree had been repeated ten times since the night of the burial at its foot, when there was a great thunderstorm over this place. It broke at midnight and raged until morning. The first intelligence he heard from his old servingman that morning was that the tree had been struck by Lightning.

"It had been riven down the stem in a very surprising manner, and the stem lay in two blighted shafts: one resting against the house and one against a portion of the old red garden wall, in which its fall had made a gap. The fissure went down the tree to a little above the earth, and there stopped. There was great curiosity to see the tree and, with most of his former fears revived, he sat in his arbour – grown quite an old man – watching the people who came to see it.

"They quickly began to come in such dangerous numbers that he closed his garden gate and refused to admit any more. But there were certain men of science who travelled from a distance to examine the tree, and in an evil hour he let them in – Blight and Murrain on them – let them in!

"They wanted to dig up the ruin by the roots and closely examine it, and the earth about it. Never, while he lived! They offered money for it. They! Men of science, whom he could have bought by the gross, with a scratch of his pen! He showed them the garden gate again, and locked and barred it.

"But they were bent on doing what they wanted to do, and they bribed the old servingman – a thankless wretch who regularly complained, when he received his wages, of being underpaid – and they stole into the garden by night with their lanterns, picks and shovels, and fell to at the tree. He was lying in a turret room on the other side of the house (the Bride's Chamber had been unoccupied ever since), but he soon dreamed of picks and shovels, and got up.

"He came to an upper window on that side, whence he could see their lanterns and them, and the loose earth in a heap which he had himself disturbed and put back when it was last turned to the air. It was found. They had that minute lighted on it. They were all bending over it. One of them said, 'The skull is fractured' – and another, 'See here the bones' – and another, 'See here the clothes' – and then the first struck in again and said, 'A rusty billhook!'

"He became sensible, next day, that he was already put under a strict watch, and that he could go nowhere without being followed. Before a week was out, he was taken and laid in hold. The circumstances were gradually pieced together against him with a desperate malignity and an appalling ingenuity. But see the justice of men, and how it was extended to him! He was further accused of having poisoned that girl in the Bride's Chamber. He, who had carefully and expressly avoided imperilling a hair of his head for her, and who had seen her die of her own incapacity!

"There was doubt for which of the two murders he should be first tried, but the real one was chosen, and he was found Guilty, and cast for Death. Bloodthirsty wretches! They would have made him Guilty of anything, so set they were upon having his life.

"His money could do nothing to save him, and he was hanged. *I* am He, and I was hanged at Lancaster Castle with my face to the wall, a hundred years ago!"

At this terrific announcement, Mr Goodchild tried to rise and cry out. But the two fiery lines extending from the old man's eyes to his own kept him down, and he could not utter a sound. His sense of hearing, however, was acute, and he could hear the clock strike Two. No sooner had he heard the clock strike Two, than he saw before him Two old men!

Two.

The eyes of each connected with his eyes by two films of fire, exactly like the other – each addressing him at precisely one and the same instant – each gnashing the same teeth in the same head, with the same twitched nostril above them and the same suffused expression around it. Two old men. Differing in nothing, equally distinct to the sight, the copy no fainter than the original, the second as real as the first.

"At what time," said the Two old men, "did you arrive at the door below?"

"At Six."

"And there were Six old men upon the stairs!"

Mr Goodchild having wiped the perspiration from his brow, or tried to do it, the Two old men proceeded in one voice, and in the singular number:

"I had been anatomized, but had not yet had my skeleton put together and re-hung on an iron hook, when it began to be whispered that the Bride's Chamber was haunted. It *was* haunted, and I was there.

"*We* were there. She and I were there. I, in the chair upon the hearth; she, a white wreck again, trailing itself towards me on the floor. But I was the speaker no more, and the one word that she said to me from midnight until dawn was 'Live!'

"The youth was there, likewise. In the tree outside the window. Coming and going in the moonlight, as the tree bent and gave. He has, ever since, been there, peeping in at me in my torment, revealing to me by snatches – in the pale light and slatey shadows where he comes and goes bare-headed – a billhook standing edgewise in his hair.

"In the Bride's Chamber, every night from midnight until dawn – one month in the year excepted, as I am going to tell you – he hides in the tree, and she comes towards me on the floor – always approaching – never coming nearer – always visible as if by moonlight, whether the moon shines or no – always saying, from midnight until dawn, her one word: 'Live!'

"But in the month wherein I was forced out of this life – this present month of thirty days – the Bride's Chamber is empty and quiet. Not so my old dungeon. Not so the rooms where I was restless and afraid, ten years. Both are fitfully haunted then. At One in the morning, I am what you saw me when the clock struck that hour – One old man. At Two in the morning, I am Two old men. At Three, I am Three. By Twelve at noon, I am Twelve old men. One for every hundred per cent of old gain. Every one of the Twelve, with Twelve times my old power of suffering and agony. From that hour until Twelve at night, I – Twelve old men in anguish and fearful foreboding – wait for the coming of the executioner. At Twelve at night, I – Twelve old men turned off – swing invisible outside Lancaster Castle, with Twelve faces to the wall!

"When the Bride's Chamber was first haunted, it was known to me that this punishment would never cease until I could make its nature, and my story, known to two living men together. I waited for the coming of two living men together into the Bride's Chamber years upon years. It was infused into my knowledge (of the means I am ignorant) that if two living men, with their eyes open, could be in the Bride's Chamber at One in the morning, they would see me sitting in my chair.

"At length, the whispers that the room was spiritually troubled brought two men to try the adventure. I was scarcely struck upon the hearth at midnight (I come there as if the Lightning blasted me into being), when I heard them ascending the stairs. Next, I saw them enter. One of them was a bold, gay, active man, in the prime of life, some five-and-forty years of age; the other, a dozen years younger. They brought provisions with them in a basket, and bottles. A young woman accompanied them, with wood and coals for the lighting of the fire. When she had lighted it, the bold, gay, active man accompanied her along the gallery outside the room to see her safely down the staircase, and came back laughing.

"He locked the door, examined the chamber, put out the contents of the basket on the table before the fire – little recking of me, in my appointed station on the hearth, close to him – and filled the glasses, and ate and drank. His companion did the same, and was as cheerful and confident as he – though he was the leader. When they had supped, they laid pistols on the table, turned to the fire and began to smoke their pipes of foreign make.

"They had travelled together and had been much together, and had an abundance of subjects in common. In the midst of their talking and laughing, the younger man made a reference to the leader's being always ready for any adventure – that one, or any other. He replied in these words:

"'Not quite so, Dick: if I am afraid of nothing else, I am afraid of myself.'

"His companion, seeming to grow a little dull, asked him: in what sense? How?

"'Why, thus,' he returned. 'Here is a Ghost to be disproved. Well! I cannot answer for what my fancy might do if I were alone here, or what tricks my senses might play with me if they had me to themselves. But in company with another man, and especially with you, Dick, I would consent to outface all the Ghosts that were ever told of in the universe.'

"'I had not the vanity to suppose that I was of so much importance tonight,' said the other.

"'Of so much,' rejoined the leader, more seriously than he had spoken yet, 'that I would, for the reason I have given, on no account have undertaken to pass the night here alone.'

"It was within a few minutes of One. The head of the younger man had drooped when he made his last remark, and it drooped lower now.

"'Keep awake, Dick!' said the leader, gaily. 'The small hours are the worst.'

"He tried, but his head drooped again.

"'Dick!' urged the leader. 'Keep awake!'

"'I can't,' he indistinctly muttered. 'I don't know what strange influence is stealing over me. I can't.'

"His companion looked at him with a sudden horror, and I, in my different way, felt a new horror also; it was on the stroke of One, and I felt that the second watcher was yielding to me, and that the curse was upon me that I must send him to sleep.

"'Get up and walk, Dick!' cried the leader. 'Try!'

"It was in vain to go behind the slumberer's chair and shake him. One o'clock sounded, and I was present to the elder man, and he stood transfixed before me.

"To him alone I was obliged to relate my story, without hope of benefit. To him alone I was an awful phantom making a quite useless confession. I foresee it will ever be the same. The two living men together will never come to release me. When I appear, the senses of one of the two will be locked in sleep: he will neither see nor hear me – my communication will ever be made to a solitary listener, and will ever be unserviceable. Woe! Woe! Woe!"

As the Two old men, with these words, wrung their hands, it shot into Mr Goodchild's mind that he was in the terrible situation of

being virtually alone with the spectre, and that Mr Idle's immov-
ability was explained by his having been charmed asleep at One
o'clock. In the terror of this sudden discovery, which produced an
indescribable dread, he struggled so hard to get free from the four
fiery threads that he snapped them, after he had pulled them out
to a great width. Being then out of bonds, he caught up Mr Idle
from the sofa and rushed downstairs with him.

The Haunted House*

U NDER NONE of the accredited ghostly circumstances, and environed by none of the conventional ghostly surroundings, did I first make acquaintance with the house which is the subject of this Christmas piece. I saw it in daylight, with the sun upon it. There was no wind, no rain, no lightning, no thunder, no awful or unwonted circumstance of any kind to heighten its effect. More than that, I had come to it direct from a railway station – it was not more than a mile distant from the railway station – and, as I stood outside the house, looking back upon the way I had come, I could see the goods train running smoothly along the embankment in the valley. I will not say that everything was utterly commonplace, because I doubt if anything can be that, except to utterly commonplace people – and there my vanity steps in, but I will take it on myself to say that anybody might see the house as I saw it, any fine autumn morning.

The manner of my lighting on it was this.

I was travelling towards London out of the north, intending to stop by the way to look at the house. My health required a temporary residence in the country, and a friend of mine who knew that, and who had happened to drive past the house, had written to me to suggest it as a likely place. I had got into the train at midnight, and had fallen asleep, and had woke up and had sat looking out of the window at the brilliant Northern Lights in the sky, and had fallen asleep again, and had woke up again to find the night gone, with the usual discontented conviction on me that I hadn't been to sleep at all – upon which question, in the first imbecility of that condition, I am ashamed to believe that I would have done wager by battle with the man who sat opposite me. That opposite man had had, through the night – as that opposite man always has – several legs too many, and all of them too long. In addition to this unreasonable conduct (which was only to be expected of him), he had had a pencil and a pocketbook, and had been perpetually listening and taking notes. It had appeared to me that these aggravating notes related to the jolts and bumps of the carriage, and I should have resigned myself to his taking them, under a general supposition that he was in the civil-engineering way of life, if he had not sat staring straight over my head whenever he listened. He was a goggle-eyed gentleman of a perplexed aspect, and his demeanour became unbearable.

It was a cold, dead morning (the sun not being up yet), and when I had out-watched the paling light of the fires of the iron country, and the curtain of heavy smoke that hung at once between me and the stars and between me and the day, I turned to my fellow traveller and said:

"I *beg* your pardon, sir, but do you observe anything particular in me?" For, really, he appeared to be taking down either my travelling cap or my hair, with a minuteness that was a liberty.

The goggle-eyed gentleman withdrew his eyes from behind me, as if the back of the carriage were a hundred miles off, and said, with a lofty look of compassion for my insignificance:

"In you, sir?... B."

"B, sir?" said I, growing warm.

"I have nothing to do with you, sir," returned the gentleman; "pray let me listen... O."

He enunciated this vowel after a pause, and noted it down.

At first I was alarmed, for an express lunatic and no communication with the guard is a serious position. The thought came to my relief that the gentleman might be what is popularly called a rapper: one of a sect for (some of) whom I have the highest respect, but whom I don't believe in. I was going to ask him the question, when he took the bread out of my mouth.

"You will excuse me," said the gentleman contemptuously, "if I am too much in advance of common humanity to trouble myself at all about it. I have passed the night – as indeed I pass the whole of my time now – in spiritual intercourse."

"Oh!" said I, something snappishly.

"The conference of the night began," continued the gentleman, turning several leaves of his notebook, "with this message: 'Evil communications corrupt good manners'."

"Sound," said I, "but, absolutely new?"

"New from spirits," returned the gentleman.

I could only repeat my rather snappish "Oh!" and ask if I might be favoured with the last communication?

"'A bird in the hand,'" said the gentleman, reading his last entry with great solemnity, "'is worth two in the Bosh.'"

"Truly I am of the same opinion," said I, "but shouldn't it be Bush?"

"It came to me, Bosh," returned the gentleman.

The gentleman then informed me that the spirit of Socrates had delivered this special revelation in the course of the night. "My friend, I hope you are pretty well. There are two in this railway carriage. How do you do? There are 17,479 spirits here, but you cannot see them. Pythagoras is here. He is not at liberty to mention it, but hopes you like travelling." Galileo had likewise dropped in, with this scientific intelligence. "I am glad to see you, *amico. Come sta?* Water will freeze when it is cold enough. *Addio!*" In the course of the night, also, the following phenomena had occurred. Bishop Butler had insisted on spelling his name "Bubler", for which offence against orthography and good manners he had been dismissed as out of temper. John Milton (suspected of wilful mystification) had repudiated the authorship of *Paradise Lost*, and had introduced, as joint authors of that poem, two unknown gentlemen, respectively named Grungers and Scadgingtone. And Prince Arthur, nephew of King John of England, had described himself as tolerably comfortable in the seventh circle, where he was learning to paint on velvet, under the direction of Mrs Trimmer and Mary Queen of Scots.

If this should meet the eye of the gentleman who favoured me with these disclosures, I trust he will excuse me for confessing that the sight of the rising sun, and the contemplation of the magnificent order of the vast universe, made me impatient of them. In a word, I was so impatient of them, that I was mightily glad to get out at the next station, and to exchange these clouds and vapours for the free air of heaven.

By that time it was a beautiful morning. As I walked away among such leaves as had already fallen from the golden, brown and russet trees, and as I looked around me on the wonders of Creation, and thought of the steady, unchanging and harmonious laws by which they are sustained, the gentleman's spiritual intercourse seemed to me as poor a piece of journey-work as ever this world saw. In which heathen state of mind, I came within view of the house, and stopped to examine it attentively.

It was a solitary house, standing in a sadly neglected garden: a pretty even square of some two acres. It was a house of about the time of George II; as stiff, as cold, as formal, and in as bad taste, as could possibly be desired by the most loyal admirer of the whole quartet of Georges. It was uninhabited, but had, within a year or two, been cheaply repaired to render it habitable; I say cheaply, because the work had been done in a surface manner, and was already decaying as to the paint and plaster, though the colours were fresh. A lopsided board drooped over the garden wall, announcing that it was "to let on very reasonable terms, well furnished". It was much too closely and heavily shadowed by trees, and, in particular, there were six tall poplars before the front windows, which were excessively melancholy, and the site of which had been extremely ill chosen.

It was easy to see that it was an avoided house – a house that was shunned by the village, to which my eye was guided by a church spire some half a mile off – a house that nobody would take. And the natural inference was that it had the reputation of being a haunted house.

No period within the four-and-twenty hours of day and night is so solemn to me as the early morning. In the summertime, I often rise very early, and I am always on those occasions deeply impressed by the stillness and solitude around me. Besides that there is something awful in the being surrounded by familiar faces asleep – in the knowledge that those who are dearest to us, and to whom we are dearest, are profoundly unconscious of us, in an impassive state anticipative of that mysterious condition to which we are all tending – the stopped life, the broken threads of yesterday, the deserted seat, the closed book, the unfinished but abandoned occupation, all are images of death. The tranquillity of the hour is the tranquillity of death. The colour and the chill have the same association. Even a certain air that familiar household objects take upon them when they first emerge from the shadows of the night into the morning, of being newer, and as they used to be long ago, has its counterpart in the subsidence of the worn face of maturity or age, in death, into the old youthful look. Moreover, I once saw the apparition of my father at this hour. He was alive and well, and nothing ever came of it, but I saw him in the daylight, sitting with his back towards me, on a seat that stood beside my bed. His head was resting on his hand, and whether he was slumbering or grieving, I could not discern. Amazed to see him there, I sat up, moved my position, leant out of bed and watched him. As he did not move, I spoke to him more than once. As he did not move then, I became alarmed and laid my hand upon his shoulder, as I thought – and there was no such thing.

For all these reasons, and for others less easily and briefly state-able, I find the early morning to be my most ghostly time. Any house would be more or less haunted, to me, in the early morning, and a haunted house could scarcely address me to greater advantage than then.

I walked on into the village, with the desertion of this house upon my mind, and I found the landlord of the little inn sanding his door-step. I bespoke breakfast, and broached the subject of the house.

"Is it haunted?" I asked.

The landlord looked at me, shook his head and answered, "I say nothing."

"Then it *is* haunted?"

"Well!" cried the landlord, in an outburst of frankness that had the appearance of desperation. "I wouldn't sleep in it."

"Why not?"

"If I wanted to have all the bells in a house ring, with nobody to ring 'em, and all the doors in a house bang with nobody to bang 'em, and all sorts of feet treading about with no feet there, why then," said the landlord, "I'd sleep in that house."

"Is anything seen there?"

The landlord looked at me again, and then, with his former appearance of desperation, called down his stable-yard or "Ikey!"

The call produced a high-shouldered young fellow, with a round red face, a short crop of sandy hair, a very broad humorous mouth, a turned-up nose and a great sleeved waistcoat of purple bars with mother-of-pearl buttons, that seemed to be growing upon him, and to be in a fair way – if it were not pruned – of covering his head and overrunning his boots.

"This gentleman wants to know," said the landlord, "if anything's seen at The Poplars."

"'Ooded woman with a howl," said Ikey, in a state of great freshness.

"Do you mean a cry?"

"I mean a bird, sir."

"A hooded woman with an owl. Dear me! Did you ever see her?"

"I seen the howl."

"Never the woman?"

"Not so plain as the howl, but they always keeps together."

"Has anybody ever seen the woman as plainly as the owl?"

"Lord bless you, sir! Lots."

"Who?"

"Lord bless you, sir! Lots."

"The general-dealer opposite, for instance, who is opening his shop?"

"Perkins? Bless you, Perkins wouldn't go a-nigh the place. No!" observed the young man, with considerable feeling. "He an't otherwise, an't Perkins, but an't such a fool as *that*."

(Here, the landlord murmured his confidence in Perkins's knowing better.)

"Who is – or who was – the hooded woman with the owl? Do you know?"

"Well!" said Ikey, holding up his cap with one hand while he scratched his head with the other. "They say, in general, that she was murdered, and the howl he 'ooted the while."

This very concise summary of the facts was all I could learn, except that a young man, as hearty and likely a young man as ever I see, had been took with fits and held down in 'em, after seeing the hooded woman. Also, that a personage dimly described as "a hold chap, a sort of a one-eyed tramp, answering to the name of Joby, unless you challenged him as Greenwood, and then he said, 'Why not? And even if so, mind your own business,'" had encountered the hooded woman a matter of five or six times. But I was not materially assisted by these witnesses; inasmuch as the first was in California, and the last was, as Ikey said (and he was confirmed by the landlord), "Anywheres".

Now, although I regard with a hushed and solemn fear the mysteries between which and this state of existence is interposed the barrier of the great trial and change that fall on all the things that live, and although I have not the audacity to pretend that I know anything of them, I can no more reconcile the mere banging of doors, ringing of bells, creaking of boards and suchlike insignificances, with all the majestic beauty and pervading analogy of all the divine rules that I am permitted to understand, than I had been able, a little while before, to yoke the spiritual intercourse of my fellow traveller to the chariot of the rising sun. Moreover, I had lived in two haunted houses – both abroad. In one of these, an old Italian palace, which bore the reputation of being very badly haunted indeed, and which had recently been twice abandoned on that account, I lived eight months, most tranquilly and pleasantly: notwithstanding that the house had a score of mysterious bedrooms, which were never used, and possessed, in one large room in which I sat reading, times out of number at all hours, and next to which I slept, a haunted chamber of the first pretensions. I gently hinted these considerations to the landlord. And as to this particular house having a bad name, I reasoned with him, why, how many things had bad names undeservedly, and how easy it was to give bad names, and did he not think that if he and I were persistently to whisper in the village that any weird-looking old drunken tinker of the neighbourhood had sold himself to the Devil, he would come in time to be suspected of that commercial venture! All this wise talk was perfectly ineffective with the landlord, I am bound to confess, and was as dead a failure as ever I made in my life.

To cut this part of the story short, I was piqued about the haunted house, and was already half resolved to take it. So, after breakfast, I got the keys from Perkins's brother-in-law (a whip and harness maker, who keeps the post office, and is under submission to a most rigorous wife of the Doubly Seceding Little Emmanuel persuasion) and went up to the house, attended by my landlord and by Ikey.

Within, I found it, as I had expected, transcendently dismal. The slowly changing shadows, waved on it from the heavy trees, were doleful in the last degree; the house was ill-placed, ill-built, ill-planned and ill-fitted. It was damp, it was not free from dry rot, there was a flavour of rats in it, and it was the gloomy victim of that indescribable decay which settles on all the work of man's hands whenever it is not turned to man's account. The kitchens and offices were too large and too remote from each other. Above stairs and below, waste tracks of passage intervened between patches of fertility represented by rooms, and there was a mouldy old well with a green growth upon it, hiding, like a murderous trap, near the bottom of the back stairs, under the double row of bells. One of these bells was labelled, on a black ground in faded white letters, MASTER B. This, they told me, was the bell that rang most.

"Who was Master B.?" I asked. "Is it known what he did while the owl hooted?"

"Rang the bell," said Ikey.

I was rather struck by the prompt dexterity with which this young man pitched his fur cap at the bell, and rang it himself. It was a loud, unpleasant bell, and made a very disagreeable sound. The other bells were inscribed, according to the names of the rooms to which their wires were conducted, as "Picture Room", "Double Room", "Clock Room" and the like. Following Master B.'s bell to its source, I found that young gentleman to have had but indifferent third-class accommodation in a triangular cabin under the cock-loft, with a corner fireplace which Master B. must have been exceedingly small if he were ever able to warm himself at, and a corner chimney piece like a pyramidal staircase to the ceiling for Tom Thumb. The papering of one side of the room had dropped down bodily, with fragments of plaster adhering to it, and almost blocked up the door. It appeared that Master B., in his spiritual condition, always made a point of pulling the paper down. Neither the landlord nor Ikey could suggest why he made such a fool of himself.

Except that the house had an immensely large rambling loft at top, I made no other discoveries. It was modestly well furnished, but sparely. Some of the furniture – say, a third – was as old as the house; the rest was of various periods within the last half century. I was referred to a corn-chandler in the marketplace of the country town to treat for the house. I went that day, and I took it for six months.

It was just the middle of October when I moved in with my maiden sister (I venture to call her eight-and-thirty, she is so very, very handsome, sensible and engaging). We took with us a deaf stableman, my blood-hound Turk, two woman servants and a young person called an Odd Girl. I have reason to record of the attendant last enumerated, who was one of Saint Lawrence's Union Female Orphans, that she was a fatal mistake and a disastrous engagement.

The year was dying early, the leaves were falling fast, it was a raw cold day when we took possession, and the gloom of the house was most depressing. The cook (an amiable woman, but of a weak turn of intellect) burst into tears on beholding the kitchen, and requested that her silver watch might be delivered over to her sister (2 Tuppintock's Gardens, Ligg's Walk, Clapham Rise), in the event of anything happening to her from the damp. Streaker, the housemaid, feigned cheerfulness, but was the greater martyr. The Odd Girl, who had never been in the country, alone was pleased, and made arrangements for sowing an acorn in the garden outside the scullery window, and rearing an oak.

We went, before dark, through all the natural – as opposed to super-natural – miseries incidental to our state. Dispiriting reports ascended (like the smoke) from the basement in volumes, and descended from the upper rooms. There was no rolling pin, there was no salamander (which failed to surprise me, for I don't know what it is), there was nothing in the house; what there was, was broken, the last people must have lived like pigs, what could the meaning of the landlord be? Through these distresses, the Odd Girl was cheerful and exemplary. But within four hours after dark we had got into a supernatural groove, and the Odd Girl had seen "Eyes", and was in hysterics.

My sister and I had agreed to keep the haunting strictly to ourselves, and my impression was, and still is, that I had not left Ikey, when he helped to unload the cart, alone with the women, or any one of them, for one minute. Nevertheless, as I say, the Odd Girl had "seen Eyes" (no other explanation could ever be drawn from her) before nine, and by ten o'clock had had as much vinegar applied to her as would pickle a handsome salmon.

I leave a discerning public to judge of my feelings, when, under these untoward circumstances, at about half-past ten o'clock Master B.'s bell began to ring in a most infuriated manner, and Turk howled until the house resounded with his lamentations!

I hope I may never again be in a state of mind so unchristian as the mental frame in which I lived for some weeks, respecting the memory of Master B. Whether his bell was rung by rats, or mice, or bats, or wind, or what other accidental vibration, or sometimes by one cause, sometimes another and sometimes by collusion, I don't know, but certain it is that it did ring, two nights out of three, until I conceived the happy idea of twisting Master B.'s neck – in other words, breaking his bell short off – and silencing that young gentleman, as to my experience and belief, for ever.

But by that time, the Odd Girl had developed such improving powers of catalepsy that she had become a shining example of that very inconvenient disorder. She would stiffen like a Guy Fawkes endowed with unreason, on the most irrelevant occasions. I would address the servants in a lucid manner, pointing out to them that I had painted Master B.'s room and balked the paper, and taken Master B.'s bell away and balked the ringing, and if they could suppose that that confounded boy had lived and died, to clothe himself with no better behaviour than would most unquestionably have brought him and the sharpest particles of a birch broom into close acquaintance in the present imperfect state of existence, could they also suppose a mere poor human being, such as I was, capable by those contemptible means of counteracting and limiting the powers of the disembodied spirits of the dead, or of any spirits? I say I would become emphatic and cogent, not to say rather complacent, in such an address, when it would all go for nothing by reason of the Odd Girl's suddenly stiffening from the toes upwards, and glaring among us like a parochial petrifaction.

Streaker, the housemaid, too, had an attribute of a most discomfiting nature. I am unable to say whether she was of an unusually lymphatic temperament, or what else was the matter with her, but this young woman became a mere distillery for the production of the largest and most transparent tears I ever met with. Combined with these characteristics was a peculiar tenacity of hold in those specimens, so that they didn't fall, but hung upon her face and nose. In this condition, and mildly and deploringly shaking her head, her silence would throw me more heavily than the Admirable Crichton* could have done in a verbal disputation for a purse of money. Cook, likewise, always covered me with confusion as with a garment, by neatly winding up the session with the protest that the 'ouse was wearing her out, and by meekly repeating her last wishes regarding her silver watch.

As to our nightly life, the contagion of suspicion and fear was among us, and there is no such contagion under the sky. Hooded woman? According to the accounts, we were in a perfect convent of hooded women. Noises? With that contagion downstairs, I myself have sat in the dismal parlour, listening, until I have heard so many and such strange noises, that they would have chilled my blood if I had not warmed it by dashing out to make discoveries. Try this in bed, in the dead of night; try this at your own comfortable fireside, in the life of the night. You can fill any house with noises, if you will, until you have a noise for every nerve in your nervous system.

I repeat: the contagion of suspicion and fear was among us, and there is no such contagion under the sky. The women (their noses in a chronic state of excoriation from smelling salts), were always primed and loaded for a swoon, and ready to go off with hair-triggers. The two elder detached the Odd Girl on all expeditions that were considered doubly hazardous, and she always established the reputation of such adventures by coming back cataleptic. If Cook or Streaker went overhead after dark, we knew we should presently hear a bump on the ceiling, and this took place so constantly that it was as if a fighting man were engaged to go about the house, administering a touch of his art which I believe is called The Auctioneer to every domestic he met with.

It was in vain to do anything. It was in vain to be frightened, for the moment in one's own person, by a real owl, and then to show the owl. It was in vain to discover, by striking an accidental discord on the piano, that Turk always howled at particular notes and combinations. It was in vain to be a Rhadamanthus* with the bells, and if an unfortunate bell rang without leave, to have it down inexorably and silence it. It was in vain to fire up chimneys, let torches down the well, charge furiously into suspected rooms and recesses. We changed servants, and it was no better. The new set ran away, and a third set came, and it was no better. At last, our comfortable housekeeping got to be so disorganised and wretched that I one night dejectedly said to my sister:

"Patty, I begin to despair of our getting people to go on with us here, and I think we must give this up."

My sister, who is a woman of immense spirit, replied, "No, John, don't give it up. Don't be beaten, John. There is another way."

"And what is that?" said I.

"John," returned my sister, "if we are not to be driven out of this house, and that for no reason whatever that is apparent to you or me, we must help ourselves and take the house wholly and solely into our own hands."

"But the servants…" said I.

"Have no servants," said my sister boldly.

Like most people in my grade of life, I had never thought of the possibility of going on without those faithful obstructions. The notion was so new to me when suggested that I looked very doubtful.

"We know they come here to be frightened and infect one another, and we know they are frightened and do infect one another," said my sister.

"With the exception of Bottles," I observed, in a meditative tone.

(The deaf stableman. I kept him in my service, and still keep him, as a phenomenon of moroseness not to be matched in England.)

"To be sure, John," assented my sister, "except Bottles. And what does that go to prove? Bottles talks to nobody, and hears nobody unless he is absolutely roared at, and what alarm has Bottles ever given or taken! None."

This was perfectly true; the individual in question having retired, every night at ten o'clock, to his bed over the coach house, with no other company than a pitchfork and a pail of water. That the pail of water would have been over me, and the pitchfork through me, if I had put myself without announcement in Bottles's way after that minute, I had deposited in my own mind as a fact worth remembering. Neither had Bottles ever taken the least notice of any of our many uproars. An imperturbable and speechless man, he had sat at his supper, with Streaker present in a swoon, and the Odd Girl marble, and had only put another potato in his cheek, or profited by the general misery to help himself to beefsteak pie.

"And so," continued my sister, "I exempt Bottles. And considering, John, that the house is too large, and perhaps too lonely, to be kept well in hand by Bottles, you and me, I propose that we cast among our friends for a certain selected number of the most reliable and willing, form a society here for three months, wait upon ourselves and one another, live cheerfully and socially and see what happens."

I was so charmed with my sister that I embraced her on the spot, and went into the plan with the greatest ardour.

We were then in the third week of November, but we took our measures so vigorously, and were so well seconded by the friends in whom we confided, that there was still a week of the month unexpired when our party all came down together merrily, and mustered in the haunted house.

I will mention in this place two small changes that I made while my sister and I were yet alone. It occurring to me as not improbable that Turk howled in the house at night partly because he wanted to get out of it, I stationed him in his kennel outside, but unchained, and I seriously warned the village that any man who came in his way must not expect to leave without a rip in his own throat. I then casually asked Ikey if he were a judge of a gun. On his saying, "Yes, sir, I knows a good gun when I sees her," I begged the favour of his stepping up to the house and looking at mine.

"*She's* a true one, sir," said Ikey, after inspecting a double-barrelled rifle that I bought in New York a few years ago. "No mistake about *her*, sir."

"Ikey," said I, "don't mention it; I have seen something in this house."

"No, sir?" he whispered, greedily opening his eyes. "'Ooded lady, sir?"

"Don't be frightened," said I. "It was a figure rather like you."

"Lord, sir?"

"Ikey!" said I, shaking hands with him warmly – I may say affectionately – "if there is any truth in these ghost stories, the greatest service I can do you is to fire at that figure. And I promise you, by heaven and earth, I will do it with this gun if I see it again!"

The young man thanked me, and took his leave with some little precipitation, after declining a glass of liquor. I imparted my secret to him because I had never quite forgotten his throwing his cap at the bell; because I had, on another occasion, noticed something very like a fur cap, lying not far from the bell, one night when it had burst out ringing, and because I had remarked that we were at our ghostliest whenever he came up in the evening to comfort the servants. Let me do Ikey no injustice. He was afraid of the house, and believed in its being haunted, and yet he would play false on the haunting side, so surely as he got an opportunity. The Odd Girl's case was exactly similar. She went about the house in a state of real terror, and yet lied monstrously and wilfully, and invented many of the alarms she spread, and made many of the sounds we heard. I had had my eye on the two, and I know it. It is not necessary for me, here, to account for this preposterous state of mind; I content myself with remarking that it is familiarly known to every intelligent man who has had a fair medical, legal or other watchful experience; that it is as well established and as common a state of mind as any with which observers are acquainted, and that it is one of the first elements, above all others, rationally to be suspected in, and strictly looked for, and separated from, any question of this kind.

To return to our party. The first thing we did when we were all assembled was to draw lots for bedrooms. That done, and every bedroom, and indeed, the whole house, having been minutely examined by the whole body, we allotted the various household duties, as if we had been on a gypsy party, or a yachting party, or a hunting party, or were shipwrecked. I then recounted the floating rumours concerning the hooded lady, the owl and Master B., with others, still more filmy, which had floated about during our occupation, relative to some ridiculous old ghost of a round table, and also to an impalpable Jackass, whom nobody was ever able to catch. Some of these ideas I really believe our people below had communicated to one another in some diseased way without conveying them in words. We then gravely called one another to witness that we were not there to be deceived, or to deceive – which we considered pretty much the same thing – and that, with a serious sense of responsibility, we would be strictly true to one another, and would strictly follow out the truth. The understanding was established that anyone who heard unusual noises in the night, and who wished to trace them, should knock at my door; lastly, that on Twelfth Night, the last day of the holy Christmas, all our individual experiences since that then present hour of our coming together in the haunted house should be brought to light for the good of all, and that we would hold our peace on the subject till then, unless on some remarkable provocation to break silence.

We were in number and in character, as follows:

First – to get my sister and myself out of the way – there were we two. In the drawing of lots, my sister drew her own room, and I drew Master B.'s. Next there was our first cousin John Herschel, so called after the great astronomer – than whom, I suppose, a better man at a telescope does not breathe. With him was his wife:

CHARLES DICKENS · SUPERNATURAL SHORT STORIES

a charming creature to whom he had been married in the previous spring. I thought it (under the circumstances) rather imprudent to bring her, because there is no knowing what even a false alarm may do at such a time, but I suppose he knew his own business best, and I must say that if she had been *my* wife, I never could have left her endearing and bright face behind. They drew the Clock Room. Alfred Starling, an uncommonly agreeable young fellow of eight-and-twenty for whom I have the greatest liking, was in the Double Room: mine, usually, and designated by that name from having a dressing room within it, with two large and cumbersome windows which no wedges I was ever able to make would keep from shaking in any weather, wind or no wind. Alfred is a young fellow who pretends to be "fast" (another word for loose, as I understand the term), but who is much too good and sensible for that nonsense, and who would have distinguished himself before now if his father had not unfortunately left him a small independence of two hundred a year, on the strength of which his only occupation in life has been to spend six. I am in hopes, however, that his banker may break, or that he may enter into some speculation guaranteed to pay twenty per cent, for I am convinced that if he could only be ruined, his fortune is made. Belinda Bates, bosom friend of my sister, and a most intellectual, amiable and delightful girl, got the Picture Room. She has a fine genius for poetry, combined with real business earnestness, and "goes in" – to use an expression of Alfred's – for Woman's mission, Woman's rights, Woman's wrongs and everything that is Woman's with a capital W, or is not and ought to be. "Most praiseworthy, my dear, and Heaven prosper you!" I whispered to her on the first night of my taking leave of her at the Picture Room door. "But don't overdo it. And in respect of the great necessity there is, my darling, for more employments being within the reach of Woman than our civilization has as yet assigned to her, don't fly at the unfortunate men, even those men who are at first sight in your way, as if they were the natural oppressors of your sex; for, trust me, Belinda, they do sometimes spend their wages among wives and daughters, sisters, mothers, aunts and grandmothers, and the play is, really, not *all* Wolf and Red Riding Hood, but has other parts in it." However, I digress.

Belinda, as I have mentioned, occupied the Picture Room. We had but three other chambers: the Corner Room, the Cupboard Room and the Garden Room. My old friend, Jack Governor, "slung his hammock", as he called it, in the Corner Room. I have always regarded Jack as the finest-looking sailor that ever sailed. He is grey now, but as handsome as he was a quarter of a century ago – nay, handsomer. A portly, cheery, well-built figure of a broad-shouldered man, with a frank smile, a brilliant dark eye and a rich dark eyebrow. I remember those under darker hair, and they look all the better for the silver setting. He has been wherever his Union namesake flies, has Jack, and I have met old shipmates of his, away in the Mediterranean and on the other side of the Atlantic, who have beamed and brightened at the casual mention of his name, and have cried, "You know Jack Governor? Then you know a prince of men!" That he is! And so unmistakably a naval officer, that if you were to meet him coming out of an Eskimo snow hut in sealskin, you would be vaguely persuaded he was in full naval uniform.

Jack once had that bright clear eye of his on my sister, but it fell out that he married another lady and took her to South America, where she died. This was a dozen years ago or more. He brought down with him to our haunted house a little cask of salt beef, for he is always convinced that all salt beef not of his own pickling is mere carrion, and invariably, when he goes to London, packs a piece in his portmanteau. He had also volunteered to bring with him one "Nat Beaver", an old comrade of his, captain of a merchantman. Mr Beaver, with a thickset wooden face and figure, and apparently as hard as a block all over, proved to be an intelligent man, with a world of watery experiences in him, and great practical knowledge. At times, there was a curious nervousness about him, apparently the lingering result of some old illness, but it seldom lasted many minutes. He got the Cupboard Room, and lay there next to Mr Undery, my friend and solicitor, who came down, in an amateur capacity, "to go through with it", as he said, and who plays whist better than the whole Law List, from the red cover at the beginning to the red cover at the end.

I never was happier in my life, and I believe it was the universal feeling among us. Jack Governor, always a man of wonderful resources, was chief cook, and made some of the best dishes I ever ate, including unapproachable curries. My sister was pastry cook and confectioner. Starling and I were cook's mate, turn and turn about, and on special occasions the chief cook "pressed" Mr Beaver. We had a great deal of outdoor sport and exercise, but nothing was neglected within, and there was no ill humour or misunderstanding among us, and our evenings were so delightful that we had at least one good reason for being reluctant to go to bed.

We had a few night alarms in the beginning. On the first night, I was knocked up by Jack with a most wonderful ship's lantern in his hand, like the gills of some monster of the deep, who informed me that he was "going aloft to the main truck", to have the weathercock down. It was a stormy night and I remonstrated, but Jack called my attention to its making a sound like a cry of despair, and said somebody would be "hailing a ghost" presently, if it wasn't done. So, up to the top of the house, where I could hardly stand for the wind, we went, accompanied by Mr Beaver, and there Jack, lantern and all with Mr Beaver after him, swarmed up to the top of a cupola, some two dozen feet above the chimneys, and stood upon nothing particular, coolly knocking the weathercock off, until they both got into such good spirits with the wind and the height that I thought they would never come down. Another night, they turned out again, and had a chimney cowl off. Another night, they found something else. On several occasions, they both, in the coolest manner, simultaneously dropped out of their respective bedroom windows, hand over hand by their counterpanes, to "overhaul" something mysterious in the garden.

The engagement among us was faithfully kept, and nobody revealed anything. All we knew was, if anyone's room were haunted, no one looked the worse for it. Christmas came, and we had noble Christmas fare ("all hands" had been pressed for the pudding), and Twelfth Night came, and our store of mincemeat was ample to hold out to the last day of our time, and our cake was quite a glorious sight. It was then, as we all sat round the table and the fire, that I recited the terms of our compact, and called first for...

[*Here follow ghost stories by Hesba Stretton, George Augustus Sala, Adelaide Anne Procter and Wilkie Collins, and after these the story below, by Charles Dickens:*]

THE GHOST IN MASTER B.'S ROOM

It being now my own turn, I "took the word", as the French say, and went on:

When I established myself in the triangular garret which had gained so distinguished a reputation, my thoughts naturally turned to Master B. My speculations about him were uneasy and manifold. Whether his Christian name was Benjamin, Bissextile (from his having been born in Leap Year), Bartholomew or Bill. Whether the initial letter belonged to his family name, and that was Baxter, Black, Brown, Barker, Buggins, Baker or Bird. Whether he was a foundling, and had been baptized B. Whether he was a lion-hearted boy, and B. was short for Briton, or for Bull. Whether he could possibly have been kith and kin to an illustrious lady who brightened my own childhood, and had come to the blood of the brilliant Mother Bunch?

With these profitless meditations I tormented myself much. I also carried the mysterious letter into the appearance and pursuits of the deceased, wondering whether he dressed in Blue, wore Boots (he couldn't have been Bald), was a boy of Brains, liked Books, was good at Bowling, had any skill as a Boxer, ever in his Buoyant Boyhood Bathed from a Bathing machine at Bognor, Bangor, Bournemouth, Brighton or Broadstairs, like a Bounding Billiard Ball?

So, from the first, I was haunted by the letter B.

It was not long before I remarked that I never by any hazard had a dream of Master B., or of anything belonging to him. But the instant I awoke from sleep, at whatever hour of the night, my thoughts took him up, and roamed away, trying to attach his initial letter to something that would fit it and keep it quiet.

For six nights, I had been worried thus in Master B.'s room, when I began to perceive that things were going wrong.

The first appearance that presented itself was early in the morning, when it was but just daylight and no more. I was standing shaving at my glass, when I suddenly discovered, to my consternation and amazement, that I was shaving – not myself – I am fifty – but a boy. Apparently Master B.?

I trembled and looked over my shoulder – nothing there. I looked again in the glass, and distinctly saw the features and expression of a boy, who was shaving, not to get rid of a beard, but to get one. Extremely troubled in my mind, I took a few turns in the room, and went back to the looking glass, resolved to steady my hand and complete the operation in which I had been disturbed. Opening my eyes, which I had shut while recovering my firmness, I now met in the glass, looking straight at me, the eyes of a young man of four- or five-and-twenty. Terrified by this new ghost, I closed my eyes, and made a strong effort to recover myself. Opening them again, I saw, shaving his cheek in the glass, my father, who has long been dead. Nay, I even saw my grandfather too, whom I never did see in my life.

Although naturally much affected by these remarkable visitations, I determined to keep my secret, until the time agreed upon for the present general disclosure. Agitated by a multitude of curious thoughts, I retired to my room, that night, prepared to encounter some new experience of a spectral character. Nor was my preparation needless, for, waking from an uneasy sleep at exactly two o'clock in the morning, what were my feelings to find that I was sharing my bed with the skeleton of Master B.!

I sprang up, and the skeleton sprang up also. I then heard a plaintive voice saying, "Where am I? What is become of me?" and, looking hard in that direction, perceived the ghost of Master B.

The young spectre was dressed in an obsolete fashion – or rather, was not so much dressed as put into a case of inferior pepper-and-salt cloth, made horrible by means of shining buttons. I observed that these buttons went, in a double row, over each shoulder of the young ghost, and appeared to descend his back. He wore a frill round his neck. His right hand (which I distinctly noticed to be inky) was laid upon his stomach; connecting this action with some feeble pimples on his countenance, and his general air of nausea, I concluded this ghost to be the ghost of a boy who had habitually taken a great deal too much medicine.

"Where am I?" said the little spectre, in a pathetic voice. "And why was I born in the calomel days, and why did I have all that calomel given me?"

I replied, with sincere earnestness, that upon my soul I couldn't tell him.

"Where is my little sister," said the ghost, "and where my angelic little wife, and where is the boy I went to school with?"

I entreated the phantom to be comforted, and above all things to take heart respecting the loss of the boy he went to school with. I represented to him that probably that boy never did, within human experience, come out well, when discovered. I urged that I myself had, in later life, turned up several boys whom I went to school with, and none of them had at all answered. I expressed my humble belief that that boy never did answer. I represented that he was a mythic character, a delusion and a snare. I recounted how, the last time I found him, I found him at a dinner party behind a wall of white cravat, with an inconclusive opinion on every possible subject, and a power of silent boredom absolutely titanic. I related how, on the strength of our having been together at "Old Doylance's", he had asked himself to breakfast with me (a social offence of the largest magnitude); how, fanning my weak embers of belief in Doylance's boys, I had let him in; and how he had proved to be a fearful wanderer about the earth, pursuing the race of Adam with inexplicable notions concerning the currency, and with a proposition that the Bank of England should, on pain of being abolished, instantly strike off and circulate God knows how many thousand millions of ten and sixpenny notes.

The ghost heard me in silence, and with a fixed stare. "Barber!" it apostrophized me when I had finished.

"Barber?" I repeated – for I am not of that profession.

"Condemned," said the ghost, "to shave a constant change of customers – now me – now a young man – now thyself as thou art – now thy father – now thy grandfather; condemned, too, to lie down with a skeleton every night, and to rise with it every morning…"

(I shuddered on hearing this dismal announcement).

"Barber! Pursue me!"

I had felt, even before the words were uttered, that I was under a spell to pursue the phantom. I immediately did so, and was in Master B.'s room no longer.

Most people know what long and fatiguing night journeys had been forced upon the witches who used to confess, and who, no doubt, told the exact truth – particularly as they were always assisted with leading questions, and the Torture was always ready. I asseverate that, during my occupation of Master B.'s room, I was taken by the ghost that haunted it on expeditions fully as long and wild as any of those. Assuredly, I was presented to no shabby old man with a goat's horns and tail (something between Pan and an old clothes-man), holding conventional receptions, as stupid as those of real life and less decent, but I came upon other things which appeared to me to have more meaning.

Confident that I speak the truth and shall be believed, I declare without hesitation that I followed the ghost, in the first instance on a broomstick, and afterwards on a rocking horse. The very smell of the animal's paint – especially when I brought it out, by making him warm – I am ready to swear to. I followed the ghost afterwards in a hackney coach – an institution with the peculiar smell of which the present generation is unacquainted, but to which I am again ready to swear as a combination of stable, dog with the mange and very old bellows. (In this, I appeal to previous generations to confirm or refute me.) I pursued the phantom on a headless donkey: at least, upon a donkey who was so interested in the state of his stomach that his head was always down there, investigating it; on ponies expressly born to kick up behind; on roundabouts and swings from fairs; in the first cab – another forgotten institution where the fare regularly got into bed, and was tucked up with the driver.

Not to trouble you with a detailed account of all my travels in pursuit of the ghost of Master B., which were longer and more wonderful than those of Sinbad the Sailor, I will confine myself to one experience from which you may judge of many.

I was marvellously changed. I was myself, yet not myself. I was conscious of something within me, which has been the same all through my life, and which I have always recognized under all its phases and varieties as never altering, and yet I was not the I who had gone to bed in Master B.'s room. I had the smoothest of faces and the shortest of legs, and I had taken another creature like myself, also with the smoothest of faces and the shortest of legs, behind a door, and was confiding to him a proposition of the most astounding nature.

This proposition was that we should have a seraglio.

The other creature assented warmly. He had no notion of respectability, neither had I. It was the custom of the East, it was the way of the good Caliph Haroun Alraschid (let me have the corrupted name again for once, it is so scented with sweet memories!), the usage was highly laudable, and most worthy of imitation. "Oh yes! Let us," said the other creature with a jump, "have a seraglio."

It was not because we entertained the faintest doubts of the meritorious character of the Oriental establishment we proposed to import that we perceived it must be kept a secret from Miss Griffin. It was because we knew Miss Griffin to be bereft of human sympathies, and incapable of appreciating the greatness of the great Haroun. Mystery impenetrably shrouded from Miss Griffin then, let us entrust it to Miss Bule.

We were ten in Miss Griffin's establishment by Hampstead Ponds – eight ladies and two gentlemen. Miss Bule, whom I judge to have attained a ripe age of eight or nine, took the lead in society. I opened the subject to her in the course of the day, and proposed that she should become the Favourite.

Miss Bule, after struggling with the diffidence so natural to, and charming in, her adorable sex, expressed herself as flattered by the idea, but wished to know how it was proposed to provide for Miss Pipson? Miss Bule – who was understood to have vowed towards that young lady a friendship, halves and no secrets, until death, on the *Church Service and Lessons* complete in two volumes with case and lock – Miss Bule said she could not, as the friend of Pipson, disguise from herself, or me, that Pipson was not one of the common.

Now, Miss Pipson, having curly light hair and blue eyes (which was my idea of anything mortal and feminine that was called Fair), I promptly replied that I regarded Miss Pipson in the light of the Fair Circassian.

"And what then?" Miss Bule pensively asked.

I replied that she must be inveigled by a merchant, brought to me veiled and purchased as a slave.

(The other creature had already fallen into the second male place in the state, and was set apart from Grand Vizier. He afterwards resisted this disposal of events, but had his hair pulled until he yielded.)

"Shall I be not jealous?" Miss Bule enquired, casting down her eyes.

"Zobeide, no," I replied, "you will ever be the favourite Sultana; the first place in my heart, and on my throne, will be ever yours."

Miss Bule, upon that assurance, consented to propound the idea to her seven beautiful companions. It occurring to me, in the course of the same day, that we knew we could trust a grinning and good-natured soul called Tabby, who was the serving drudge of the house, and had no more figure than one of the beds, and upon whose face there was always more or less blacklead, I slipped into Miss Bule's hand after supper a little note to that effect, dwelling on the blacklead as being in a manner deposited by the finger of Providence, pointing out for Mesrour, the celebrated chief of the Blacks of the Harem.

There were difficulties in the formation of the desired institution, as there are in all combinations. The other creature showed himself of a low character and, when defeated in aspiring to the throne, pretended to have conscientious scruples about prostrating himself before the Caliph, wouldn't call him Commander of the Faithful, spoke of him slightingly and inconsistently as a mere "chap", said he, the other creature, "wouldn't play" – play! – and was otherwise coarse and offensive. This meanness of disposition was, however, put down by the general indignation of a united seraglio, and I became blessed in the smiles of eight of the fairest of the daughters of men.

The smiles could only be bestowed when Miss Griffin was looking another way, and only then in a very wary manner, for there was a legend among the followers of the Prophet that she saw with a little round ornament in the middle of the pattern on the back of her shawl. But every day after dinner, for an hour, we were all together, and then the Favourite and the rest of the Royal Harem competed who should most beguile the leisure of the Serene Haroun reposing from the cares of state – which were generally, as in most affairs of state, of an arithmetical character, the Commander of the Faithful being a fearful boggler at a sum.

On these occasions, the devoted Mesrour, chief of the Blacks of the Harem, was always in attendance (Miss Griffin usually ringing for that officer, at the same time, with great vehemence), but never acquitted himself in a manner worthy of his historical reputation. In the first place, his bringing a broom into the divan of the Caliph, even when Haroun wore on his shoulders the red robe of anger (Miss Pipson's pelisse), though it might be got over for the moment, was never to be quite satisfactorily accounted for. In the second place, his breaking out into grinning exclamations of "Lork you pretties!" was neither Eastern nor respectful. In the third place, when specially instructed to say "Bismillah!" he always said "Hallelujah!" This officer, unlike his class, was too good-humoured altogether, kept his mouth open far too wide, expressed approbation to an incongruous extent, and even once – it was on the occasion of the purchase of the Fair Circassian for five hundred thousand purses of gold, and cheap, too – embraced the slave, the Favourite, and the Caliph, all round. (Parenthetically let me say God bless Mesrour, and may there have been sons and daughters on that tender bosom, softening many a hard day since!)

Miss Griffin was a model of propriety, and I am at a loss to imagine what the feelings of the virtuous woman would have been if she had known, when she paraded us down the Hampstead road two and two, that she was walking with a stately step at the head of Polygamy and Mahommedanism. I believe that a mysterious and terrible joy with which the contemplation of Miss Griffin, in this unconscious state, inspired us, and a grim sense prevalent among us that there was a dreadful power in our knowledge of what Miss Griffin (who knew all things that could be learnt out of a book) didn't know, were the mainspring of the preservation of our secret. It was wonderfully kept, but was once upon the verge of self-betrayal. The danger and escape occurred upon a Sunday. We were all ten ranged in a conspicuous part of the gallery at church, with Miss Griffin at our head – as we were every Sunday – advertising the establishment in an unsecular sort of way – when the description of Solomon in his domestic glory happened to be read. The moment that monarch was thus referred to, conscience whispered me, "Thou, too, Haroun!" The officiating minister had a cast in his eye, and it assisted conscience by giving him the appearance of reading personally at me. A crimson blush, attended by a fearful perspiration, suffused my features. The Grand Vizier became more dead than alive, and the whole seraglio reddened as if the sunset of Baghdad shone direct upon their lovely faces. At this portentous time the awful Griffin rose, and balefully surveyed the children of Islam. My own impression was that Church and State had entered into a conspiracy with Miss Griffin to expose us, and that we should all be put into white sheets, and exhibited in the centre aisle. But so Westerly – if I may be allowed the expression as opposite to Eastern associations – was Miss Griffin's sense of rectitude, that she merely suspected apples, and we were saved.

I have called the seraglio united. Upon the question, solely, whether the Commander of the Faithful durst exercise a right of kissing in that sanctuary of the palace, were its peerless intimates divided. Zobeide asserted a counter-right in the Favourite to scratch, and the Fair Circassian put her face, for refuge, into a green baize bag, originally designed for books. On the other hand, a young antelope of transcendent beauty from the fruitful plains of Camden Town (whence she had been brought, by traders, in the half-yearly caravan that crossed the intermediate desert after the holidays), held more liberal opinions, but stipulated for limiting the benefit of them to that dog, and son of a dog, the Grand Vizier – who had no rights, and was not in question. At length, the difficulty was compromised by the installation of a very youthful slave as deputy. She, raised upon a stool, officially received upon her cheeks the salutes intended by the gracious Haroun for other Sultanas, and was privately rewarded from the coffers of the Ladies of the Harem.

And now it was, at the full height of enjoyment of my bliss, that I became heavily troubled. I began to think of my mother, and what she would say to my taking home at midsummer eight of the most beautiful daughters of men, but all unexpected. I thought of the number of beds we made up at our house, of my father's income and of the baker, and my despondency redoubled. The seraglio and malicious Vizier, divining the cause of their Lord's unhappiness, did their utmost to augment it. They professed unbounded felicity, and declared that they would live and die with him. Reduced to the utmost wretchedness by these protestations of attachment, I lay awake, for hours at a time, ruminating on my frightful lot. In my despair, I think I might have taken an early opportunity of falling on my knees before Miss Griffin, avowing my resemblance to Solomon, and praying to be dealt with according to the outraged laws of my country, if an unthought-of means of escape had not opened before me.

One day, we were out walking, two and two – on which occasion the Vizier had his usual instructions to take note of the boy at the turnpike, and if he profanely gazed (which he always did) at the beauties of the harem, to have him bowstrung in the course of the night – and it happened that our hearts were veiled in gloom. An unaccountable action on the part of the antelope had plunged the state into disgrace. That charmer, on the representation that the previous day was her birthday, and that vast treasures had been sent in a hamper for its celebration (both baseless assertions), had secretly but most pressingly invited thirty-five neighbouring princes and princesses to a ball and supper, with a special stipulation that they were "not to be fetched till twelve". This wandering of the antelope's fancy led to the surprising arrival at Miss Griffin's door, in divers equipages and under various escorts, of a great company in full dress, who were deposited on the top step in a flush of high expectancy, and who were dismissed in tears. At the beginning of the double knocks attendant on these ceremonies, the antelope had retired to a back attic, and bolted herself in, and at every new arrival, Miss Griffin had gone so much more and more distracted, that at last she had been seen to tear her front. Ultimate capitulation on the part of the offender had been followed by solitude in the linen closet, bread and water, and a lecture to all of vindictive length, in which Miss Griffin had used the expressions: firstly, "I believe you all of you knew of it", secondly, "Every one of you is as wicked as another", thirdly, "A pack of little wretches".

Under these circumstances, we were walking drearily along, and I especially, with my Mussulman responsibilities heavy on me, was in a very low state of mind, when a strange man accosted Miss Griffin, and, after walking on at her side for a little while and talking with her, looked at me. Supposing him to be a minion of the law, and that my hour was come, I instantly ran away, with a general purpose of making for Egypt.

The whole seraglio cried out, when they saw me making off as fast as my legs would carry me (I had an impression that the first turning on the left, and round by the public house, would be the shortest way to the Pyramids), Miss Griffin screamed after me, the faithless Vizier ran after me and the boy at the turnpike dodged me into a corner, like a sheep, and cut me off. Nobody scolded me when I was taken and brought back; Miss Griffin only said, with a stunning gentleness, This was very curious! Why had I run away when the gentleman looked at me?

If I had had any breath to answer with, I dare say I should have made no answer; having no breath, I certainly made none. Miss Griffin and the strange man took me between them, and walked me back to the palace in a sort of state, but not at all (as I couldn't help feeling, with astonishment), in culprit state.

When we got there, we went into a room by ourselves, and Miss Griffin called in to her assistance Mesrour, chief of the dusky guards of the harem. Mesrour, on being whispered to, began to shed tears.

"Bless you, my precious!" said that officer, turning to me, "your Pa's took bitter bad!"

I asked, with a fluttered heart, "Is he very ill?"

"Lord temper the wind to you, my lamb!" said the good Mesrour, kneeling down, that I might have a comforting shoulder for my head to rest on. "Your Pa's dead!"

Haroun Alraschid took to flight at the words; the seraglio vanished; from that moment, I never again saw one of the eight of the fairest of the daughters of men.

I was taken home, and there was Debt at home as well as Death, and we had a sale there. My own little bed was as superciliously looked upon by a Power unknown to me, hazily called "The Trade", that a brass coal scuttle, a roasting jack and a birdcage were obliged to be put into it to make a lot of it, and then it went for a song. So I heard mentioned, and I wondered what song, and thought what a dismal song it must have been to sing!

Then I was sent to a great, cold, bare school of big boys; where everything to eat and wear was thick and clumpy, without being enough; where everybody, large and small, was cruel; where the boys knew all about the sale, before I got there, and asked me what I had fetched, and who had bought me, and hooted at me, "Going, going, gone!" I never whispered in that wretched place that I had been Haroun, or had had a seraglio – for I knew that if I mentioned my reverses, I should be so worried that I should have to drown myself in the muddy pond near the playground, which looked like the beer.

Ah me, ah me! No other ghost has haunted the boy's room, my friends, since I have occupied it, than the ghost of my own childhood, the ghost of my own innocence, the ghost of my own airy belief. Many a time have I pursued the phantom – never with this man's stride of mine to come up with it, never with these man's hands of mine to touch it, never more to this man's heart of mine to hold it in its purity. And here you see me working out, as cheerfully and thankfully as I may, my doom of shaving in the glass a constant change of customers, and of lying down and rising up with the skeleton allotted to me for my mortal companion.

[*Here follows a ghost story by Elizabeth Gaskell, and after that the short piece below – the last in the* Haunted House *collection – by Charles Dickens:*]

THE GHOST IN THE CORNER ROOM

I had observed Mr Governor growing fidgety as his turn – his "spell", he called it – approached, and he now surprised us all by rising with a serious countenance, and requesting permission to "come aft" and have speech with me, before he spun his yarn. His great popularity led to a gracious concession of this indulgence, and we went out together into the hall.

"Old shipmate," said Mr Governor to me, "ever since I have been aboard this old hulk, I have been haunted, day and night."

"By what, Jack?"

Mr Governor, clapping his hand on my shoulder and keeping it there, said:

"By something of the likeness of a woman."

"Ah! Your old affliction. You'll never get over *that*, Jack, if you live to be a hundred."

"No, don't talk so, because I am very serious. All night long, I have been haunted by one figure. All day, the same figure has so bewildered me in the kitchen, that I wonder I haven't poisoned the whole ship's company. Now, there's no fancy here. Would you like to see the figure?"

"I should like to see it very much."

"Then here it is!" said Jack. Thereupon, he presented my sister, who had stolen out quietly, after us.

"Oh, indeed?" said I. "Then, I suppose, Patty, my dear, I have no occasion to ask whether *you* have been haunted?"

"Constantly, Joe," she replied.

THE HAUNTED HOUSE

The effect of our going back again, all three together, and of my presenting my sister as the Ghost from the Corner Room, and Jack as the Ghost from my Sister's Room, was triumphant – the crowning hit of the night. Mr Beaver was so particularly delighted that he by and by declared a very little would make him dance a hornpipe. Mr Governor immediately supplied the very little by offering to make it a double hornpipe, and there ensued such toe-and-heeling, and buckle-covering, and double-shuffling, and heel-sliding, and execution of all sorts of slippery manoeuvres with vibratory legs, as none of us ever saw before, or will ever see again. When we had all laughed and applauded till we were faint, Starling, not to be outdone, favoured us with a more modern saltatory entertainment in the Lancashire clog manner – to the best of my belief, the longest dance ever performed – in which the sound of his feet became a locomotive going through cuttings, tunnels and open country, and became a vast number of other things we should never have suspected, unless he had kindly told us what they were.

It was resolved before we separated that night that our three months' period in the Haunted House should be wound up with the marriage of my sister and Mr Governor. Belinda was nominated bridesmaid, and Starling was engaged for bridegroom's man.

In a word, we lived our term out most happily, and were never for a moment haunted by anything more disagreeable than our own imaginations and remembrances. My cousin's wife, in her great love for her husband and in her gratitude to him for the change her love had wrought in her, had told us, through his lips, her own story, and I am sure there was not one of us who did not like her the better for it, and respect her the more.

So, at last, before the shortest month in the year was quite out, we all walked forth one morning to the church with the spire, as if nothing uncommon were going to happen, and there Jack and my sister were married, as sensibly as could be. It occurs to me that I observed Belinda and Alfred Starling to be rather sentimental and low, on the occasion, and they are since engaged to be married in the same church. I regard it as an excellent thing for both, and a kind of union very wholesome for the times in which we live. He wants a little poetry, and she wants a little prose, and the marriage of the two things is the happiest marriage I know for all mankind.

Finally, I derived this Christmas greeting from the Haunted House, which I affectionately address with all my heart to all my readers: – Let us use the great virtue, Faith, but not abuse it, and let us put it to its best use, by having faith in the great Christmas book of the New Testament, and in one another.

To Be Taken with a Grain of Salt*

I HAVE ALWAYS NOTICED a prevalent want of courage, even among persons of superior intelligence and culture, as to imparting their own psychological experiences when those have been of a strange sort. Almost all men are afraid that what they could relate in such wise would find no parallel or response in a listener's internal life, and might be suspected or laughed at. A truthful traveller, who should have seen some extraordinary creature in the likeness of a sea-serpent, would have no fear of mentioning it, but the same traveller, having had some singular presentiment, impulse, vagary of thought, vision (so called), dream or other remarkable mental impression, would hesitate considerably before he would own to it. To this reticence I attribute much of the obscurity in which such subjects are involved. We do not habitually communicate our experiences of these subjective things as we do our experiences of objective creation. The consequence is that the general stock of experience in this regard appears exceptional, and really is so, in respect of being miserably imperfect.

In what I am going to relate, I have no intention of setting up, opposing or supporting, any theory whatever. I know the history of the Bookseller of Berlin. I have studied the case of the wife of a late Astronomer Royal as related by Sir David Brewster,* and I have followed the minutest details of a much more remarkable case of Spectral Illusion occurring within my private circle of friends. It may be necessary to state, as to this last, that the sufferer (a lady) was in no degree, however distant, related to me. A mistaken assumption on that head might suggest an explanation of a part of my own case – but only a part – which would be wholly without foundation. It cannot be referred to my inheritance of any developed peculiarity, nor had I ever before any at all similar experience, nor have I ever had any at all similar experience since.

It does not signify how many years ago, or how few, a certain murder was committed in England which attracted great attention. We hear more than enough of murderers as they rise in succession to their atrocious eminence, and I would bury the memory of this particular brute, if I could, as his body was buried in Newgate Jail. I purposely abstain from giving any direct clue to the criminal's individuality.

When the murder was first discovered, no suspicion fell – or I ought rather to say, for I cannot be too precise in my facts, it was nowhere publicly hinted that any suspicion fell – on the man who was afterwards brought to trial. As no reference was at that time made to him in the newspapers, it is obviously impossible that any description of him can at that time have been given in the newspapers. It is essential that this fact be remembered.

Unfolding at breakfast my morning paper, containing the account of that first discovery, I found it to be deeply interesting, and I read it with close attention. I read it twice, if not three times. The discovery had been made in a bedroom, and when I laid down the paper, I was aware of a flash – rush – flow – I do not know what to call it – no word I can find is satisfactorily descriptive – in which I seemed to see that bedroom passing through my room, like a picture impossibly painted on a running river. Though almost instantaneous in its passing, it was perfectly clear – so clear that I distinctly, and with a sense of relief, observed the absence of the dead body from the bed.

It was in no romantic place that I had this curious sensation, but in chambers in Piccadilly, very near to the corner of St James's Street. It was entirely new to me. I was in my easy chair at the moment, and the sensation was accompanied with a peculiar shiver which started the chair from its position. (But it is to be noted that the chair ran easily on castors.) I went to one of the windows (there are two in the room, and the room is on the second floor) to refresh my eyes with the moving objects down in Piccadilly. It was a bright autumn morning, and the street was sparkling and cheerful. The wind was high. As I looked out, it brought down from the Park a quantity of fallen leaves, which a gust took and whirled into a spiral pillar. As the pillar fell and the leaves dispersed, I saw two men on the opposite side of the way, going from west to east. They were one behind the other. The foremost man often looked back over his shoulder. The second man followed him at a distance of some thirty paces, with his right hand menacingly raised. First the singularity and steadiness of this threatening gesture in so public a thoroughfare attracted my attention, and next the more remarkable circumstance that nobody heeded it. Both men threaded their way among the other passengers with a smoothness hardly consistent even with the action of walking on a pavement – and no single creature that I could see gave them place, touched them or looked after them. In passing before my windows, they both stared up at me. I saw their two faces very distinctly, and I knew that I could recognize them anywhere. Not that I consciously noticed anything very remarkable in either face, except that the man who went first had an unusually lowering appearance, and that the face of the man who followed him was of the colour of impure wax.

I am a bachelor, and my valet and his wife constitute my whole establishment. My occupation is in a certain Branch Bank, and I wish that my duties as head of a department were as light as they are popularly supposed to be. They kept me in town that autumn, when I stood in need of change. I was not ill, but I was not well. My reader is to make the most that can be reasonably made of my feeling jaded, having a depressing sense upon me of a monotonous life, and being "slightly dyspeptic". I am assured by my renowned doctor that my real state of health at that time justifies no stronger description, and I quote his own from his written answer to my request for it.

As the circumstances of the murder, gradually unravelling, took stronger and stronger possession of the public mind, I kept them away from mine by knowing as little about them as was possible in the midst of the universal excitement. But I knew that a verdict of wilful murder had been found against the suspected murderer, and that he had been committed to Newgate for trial. I also knew that his trial had been postponed over one Sessions of the Central Criminal Court on the ground of general prejudice and want of time for the preparation of the defence. I may further have known – but I believe I did not – when, or about when, the Sessions to which his trial stood postponed would come on.

My sitting room, bedroom and dressing room are all on one floor. With the last there is no communication but through the bedroom. True, there is a door in it, once communicating with the staircase, but a part of the fitting of my bath has been – and had then been for some years – fixed across it. At the same period, and as a part of the same arrangement, the door had been nailed up and canvassed over.

I was standing in my bedroom late one night, giving some directions to my servant before he went to bed. My face was towards the only available door of communication with the dressing room, and it was closed. My servant's back was towards that door. While I was speaking to him, I saw it open, and a man look in who very earnestly and mysteriously beckoned to me. That man was the man who had gone second of the two along Piccadilly, and whose face was the colour of impure wax.

The figure, having beckoned, drew back and closed the door. With no longer pause than was made by my crossing the bedroom, I opened the dressing-room door and looked in. I had a lighted candle already in my hand. I felt no inward expectation of seeing the figure in the dressing room, and I did not see it there.

Conscious that my servant stood amazed, I turned round to him and said: "Derrick, could you believe that in my cool senses I fancied I saw a…" As I there laid my hand upon his breast, with a sudden start he trembled violently and said: "Oh Lord, yes, sir! A dead man beckoning!"

Now I do not believe that this John Derrick, my trusty and attached servant for more than twenty years, had any impression whatever of having seen any such figure until I touched him. The change in him was so startling, when I touched him, that I fully believe he derived his impression in some occult manner from me at that instant.

I bade John Derrick bring some brandy, and I gave him a dram and was glad to take one myself. Of what had preceded that night's phenomenon, I told him not a single word. Reflecting on it, I was absolutely certain that I had never seen that face before, except on the one occasion in Piccadilly. Comparing its expression when beckoning at the door with its expression when it had stared up at me as I stood at my window, I came to the conclusion that on the first occasion it had sought to fasten itself upon my memory, and that on the second occasion it had made sure of being immediately remembered.

I was not very comfortable that night, though I felt a certainty, difficult to explain, that the figure would not return. At daylight I fell into a heavy sleep, from which I was awakened by John Derrick's coming to my bedside with a paper in his hand.

This paper, it appeared, had been the subject of an altercation at the door between its bearer and my servant. It was a summons to me to serve upon a jury at the forthcoming Sessions of the Central Criminal Court at the Old Bailey. I had never before been summoned on such a jury, as John Derrick well knew. He believed – I am not certain at this hour whether with reason or otherwise – that that class of jurors were customarily chosen on a lower qualification than mine, and he had at first refused to accept the summons. The man who served it had taken the matter very coolly. He had said that my attendance or non-attendance was nothing to him: there the summons was – and I should deal with it at my own peril, and not at his.

For a day or two I was undecided whether to respond to this call or take no notice of it. I was not conscious of the slightest mysterious bias, influence or attraction one way or other. Of that I am as strictly sure as of every other statement that I make here. Ultimately I decided, as a break in the monotony of my life, that I would go.

The appointed morning was a raw morning in the month of November. There was a dense brown fog in Piccadilly, and it became positively black and in the last degree oppressive east of Temple Bar. I found the passages and staircases of the Court House flaringly lighted with gas, and the Court itself similarly illuminated. I *think* that, until I was conducted by officers into the Old Court and saw its crowded state, I did not know that the murderer was to be tried that day. I *think* that, until I was so helped into the Old Court with considerable difficulty, I did not know into which of the two courts sitting my summons would take me. But this must not be received as a positive assertion, for I am not completely satisfied in my mind on either point.

I took my seat in the place appropriated to jurors in waiting, and I looked about the court as well as I could through the cloud of fog and breath that was heavy in it. I noticed the black vapour hanging like a murky curtain outside the great windows, and I noticed the stifled sound of wheels on the straw or tan that was littered in the street; also, the hum of the people gathered there, which a shrill whistle or a louder song or hail than the rest occasionally pierced. Soon afterwards the judges, two in number, entered and took their seats. The buzz in the court was awfully hushed. The direction was given to put the murderer to the bar. He appeared there. And in that same instant I recognized in him the first of the two men who had gone down Piccadilly.

If my name had been called then, I doubt if I could have answered to it audibly. But it was called about sixth or eighth in the panel, and I was by that time able to say "Here!" Now, observe. As I stepped into the box, the prisoner, who had been looking on attentively but with no sign of concern, became violently agitated and beckoned to his attorney. The prisoner's wish to challenge me was so manifest that it occasioned a pause, during which the attorney, with his hand upon the dock, whispered with his client and shook his head. I afterwards had it from that gentleman that the prisoner's first affrighted words to him were "*At all hazards, challenge that man*", but that – as he would give no reason for it and admitted that he had not even known my name until he heard it called and I appeared – it was not done.

Both on the ground already explained that I wish to avoid reviving the unwholesome memory of that murderer and also because a detailed account of his long trial is by no means indispensable to my narrative, I shall confine myself to such incidents in the ten days and nights during which we, the jury, were kept together as directly bear on my own curious personal experience. It is in that, and not in the murderer, that I seek to interest my reader. It is to that, and not to a page of the Newgate calendar, that I beg attention.

I was chosen foreman of the jury. On the second morning of the trial, after evidence had been taken for two hours (I heard the church clocks strike), happening to cast my eyes over my brother jurymen, I found an inexplicable difficulty in counting them. I counted them several times, yet always with the same difficulty. In short, I made them one too many.

I touched the brother juryman whose place was next me, and I whispered to him: "Oblige me by counting us." He looked surprised by the request, but turned his head and counted. "Why," says he, suddenly, "we are thirt— but no, it's not possible. No. We are twelve."

According to my counting that day, we were always right in detail, but in the gross we were always one too many. There was no appearance – no figure – to account for it, but I had now an inward foreshadowing of the figure that was surely coming.

The jury were housed at the London Tavern. We all slept in one large room on separate tables, and we were constantly in the charge and under the eye of the officer sworn to hold us in safekeeping. I see no reason for suppressing the real name of that officer. He was intelligent, highly polite and obliging, and (I was glad to hear) much respected in the City. He had an agreeable presence, good eyes, enviable black whiskers and a fine, sonorous voice. His name was Mr Harker.

When we turned into our twelve beds at night, Mr Harker's bed was drawn across the door. On the night of the second day, not being disposed to lie down and seeing Mr Harker sitting on his bed, I went and sat beside him, and offered him a pinch of snuff. As Mr Harker's hand touched mine in taking it from my box, a peculiar shiver crossed him, and he said: "Who is this?"

Following Mr Harker's eyes and looking along the room, I saw again the figure I expected – the second of the two men who had gone down Piccadilly. I rose and advanced a few steps, then stopped and looked round at Mr Harker. He was quite uncon-cerned, laughed and said in a pleasant way: "I thought for a moment we had a thirteenth juryman, without a bed. But I see it is the moonlight."

Making no revelation to Mr Harker, but inviting him to take a walk with me to the end of the room, I watched what the figure did. It stood for a few moments by the bedside of each of my eleven brother jurymen, close to the pillow. It always went to the right-hand side of the bed, and always passed out crossing the foot of the next bed. It seemed, from the action of the head, merely to look down pensively at each recumbent figure. It took no notice of me or of my bed, which was the nearest to Mr Harker's. It seemed to go out where the moonlight came in, through a high window, as by an aerial flight of stairs.

Next morning, at breakfast, it appeared that everybody present had dreamed of the murdered man last night, except myself and Mr Harker.

I now felt convinced that the second man who had gone down Piccadilly was the murdered man (so to speak), as if it had been borne into my comprehension by his immediate testimony. But even this took place, and in a manner for which I was not at all prepared.

On the fifth day of the trial, when the case for the prosecution was drawing to a close, a miniature of the murdered man, missing from his bedroom upon the discovery of the deed and afterwards found in a hiding place where the murderer had been seen digging, was put in evidence. Having been identified by the witness under examination, it was handed up to the Bench, and thence handed down to be inspected by the jury. As an officer in a black gown was making his way with it across to me, the figure of the second man who had gone down Piccadilly impetuously started from the crowd, caught the miniature from the officer and gave it to me with his own hands, at the same time saying, in a low and hollow tone – before I saw the miniature, which was in a locket: "*I was younger then, and my face was not then drained of blood.*" It also came between me and the brother juryman to whom I would have given the miniature, and between him and the brother juryman to whom he would have given it, and so passed it on through the whole of our number and back into my possession. Not one of them, however, detected this.

At table, and generally when we were shut up together in Mr Harker's custody, we had from the first naturally discussed the day's proceedings a good deal. On that fifth day, the case for the prosecution being closed, and we having that side of the question in a completed shape before us, our discussion was more animated and serious. Among our number was a vestryman – the densest idiot I have ever seen at large – who met the plainest evidence with the most preposterous objections, and who was sided with by two flabby parochial parasites – all the three impanelled from a district so delivered over to fever that they ought to have been upon their own trial for five hundred murders. When these mischievous blockheads were at their loudest, which was towards midnight, while some of us were already preparing for bed, I again saw the murdered man. He stood grimly behind them, beckoning to me. On my going towards them and striking into the conversation, he immediately retired. This was the beginning of a separate series of appearances, confined to that long room in which we were confined. Whenever a knot of my brother jurymen laid their heads together, I saw the head of the murdered man among them. Whenever their comparison of notes was going against him, he would solemnly and irresistibly beckon to me.

It will be borne in mind that down to the production of the miniature, on the fifth day of the trial, I had never seen the appearance in court. Three changes occurred now that we entered on the case for the defence. Two of them I will mention together first. The figure was now in court continually, and it never there addressed itself to me, but always to the person who was speaking at the time. For instance: the throat of the murdered man had been cut straight across. In the opening speech for the defence, it was suggested that the deceased might have cut his own throat. At that very moment the figure, with its throat in the dreadful condition referred to (this it had concealed before), stood at the speaker's elbow, motioning across and across its windpipe now with the right hand, now with the left, vigorously suggesting to the speaker himself the impossibility of such a wound having been self-inflicted by either hand. For another instance: a witness to character, a woman, deposed to the prisoner's being the most amiable of mankind. The figure at that instant stood on the floor before her, looking her full in the face and pointing out the prisoner's evil countenance with an extended arm and an outstretched finger.

The third change now to be added impressed me strongly as the most marked and striking of all. I do not theorize upon it: I accurately state it, and there leave it. Although the appearance was not itself perceived by those whom it addressed, its coming close to such persons was invariably attended by some trepidation or disturbance on their part. It seemed to me as if it were prevented, by laws to which I was not amenable, from fully revealing itself to others, and yet as if it could visibly, dumbly and darkly over-shadow their minds. When the leading counsel for the defence suggested that hypothesis of suicide, and the figure stood at the learned gentleman's elbow frightfully sawing at its severed throat, it is undeniable that the counsel faltered in his speech, lost for a few seconds the thread of his ingenious discourse, wiped his fore-head with his handkerchief and turned extremely pale. When the witness to character was confronted by the appearance, her eyes most certainly did follow the direction of its pointed finger and rest in great hesitation and trouble upon the prisoner's face. Two additional illustrations will suffice. On the eighth day of the trial, after a pause which was every day made early in the afternoon for a few minutes' rest and refreshment, I came back into court with the rest of the jury some little time before the return of the judges. Standing up in the box and looking about me, I thought the figure was not there – until, chancing to raise my eyes to the gallery, I saw it bending forward and leaning over a very decent woman, as if to assure itself whether the judges had resumed their seats or not. Immediately afterwards that woman screamed, fainted and was carried out. So with the venerable, sagacious and patient judge who conducted the trial. When the case was over and he settled himself and his papers to sum up, the murdered man, entering the judges' door, advanced to his Lordship's desk and looked eagerly over his shoulder at the pages of his notes which he was turning. A change came over his Lordship's face: his hand stopped; the peculiar shiver that I knew so well passed over him; he faltered: "Excuse me, gentlemen, for a few moments. I am somewhat oppressed by the vitiated air" – and did not recover until he had drunk a glass of water.

Through all the monotony of six of those interminable ten days – the same judges and others on the bench, the same murderer in the dock, the same lawyers at the table, the same tones of question and answer rising to the roof of the court, the same scratching of the judge's pen, the same ushers going in and out, the same lights kindled at the same hour when there had been any natural light of day, the same foggy curtain outside the great windows when it was foggy, the same rain pattering and dripping when it was rainy, the same footmarks of turnkeys and prisoner day after day on the same sawdust, the same keys locking and unlocking the same heavy doors – through all the wearisome monotony which made me feel as if I had been foreman of the jury for a vast period of time and Piccadilly had flourished coevally with Babylon, the murdered man never lost one trace of his distinctness in my eyes, nor was he at any moment less distinct than anybody else. I must not omit, as a matter of fact, that I never once saw the appearance which I call by the name of the murdered man look at the murderer. Again and again I wondered: "Why does he not?" But he never did.

Nor did he look at me, after the production of the miniature, until the last closing minutes of the trial arrived. We retired to consider at seven minutes before ten at night. The idiotic ves-tryman and his two parochial parasites gave us so much trouble that we twice returned into court to beg to have certain extracts from the judge's notes reread. Nine of us had not the smallest doubt about these passages – neither, I believe, had anyone in court; the dunder-headed triumvirate, however, having no idea but obstruction, disputed them for that very reason. At length we prevailed, and finally the jury returned into court at ten minutes past twelve.

The murdered man at that time stood directly opposite the jury box, on the other side of the court. As I took my place, his eyes rested on me with great attention; he seemed satisfied, and slowly shook a great grey veil, which he carried on his arm for the first time, over his head and whole form. As I gave in our verdict – "Guilty" – the veil collapsed, all was gone and his place was empty.

The murderer, being asked by the judge, according to usage, whether he had anything to say before sentence of Death should be passed upon him, indistinctly muttered something which was described in the leading newspapers of the following day as "a few rambling, incoherent and half-audible words in which he was understood to complain that he had not had a fair trial, because the foreman of the jury was prepossessed against him". The remarkable declaration that he really made was this: "*My Lord, I knew I was a doomed man when the foreman of my jury came into the box. My Lord, I knew he would never let me off, because before I was taken he somehow got to my bedside in the night, woke me and put a rope round my neck*".

No. 1. Branch Line: The Signalman*

"HALLOA! Below there!"

When he heard a voice thus calling to him, he was standing at the door of his box, with a flag in his hand, furled round its short pole. One would have thought, considering the nature of the ground, that he could not have doubted from what quarter the voice came; but, instead of looking up to where I stood on the top of the steep cutting nearly over his head, he turned himself about and looked down the line. There was something remarkable in his manner of doing so, though I could not have said, for my life, what. But I know it was remarkable enough to attract my notice, even though his figure was foreshortened and shadowed, down in the deep trench, and mine was high above him, so steeped in the glow of an angry sunset that I had shaded my eyes with my hand before I saw him at all.

"Halloa! Below!"

From looking down the line, he turned himself about again and, raising his eyes, saw my figure high above him.

"Is there any path by which I can come down and speak to you?"

He looked up at me without replying, and I looked down at him without pressing him too soon with a repetition of my idle question. Just then, there came a vague vibration in the earth and air, quickly changing into a violent pulsation, and an oncoming rush that caused me to start back, as though it had force to draw me down. When such vapour as rose to my height from this rapid train had passed me and was skimming away over the landscape, I looked down again and saw him refurling the flag he had shown while the train went by.

I repeated my enquiry. After a pause, during which he seemed to regard me with fixed attention, he motioned with his rolled-up flag towards a point on my level, some two or three hundred yards distant. I called down to him, "All right!" and made for that point. There, by dint of looking closely about me, I found a rough zigzag-descending path notched out – which I followed.

The cutting was extremely deep, and unusually precipitate. It was made through a clammy stone that became oozier and wetter as I went down. For these reasons, I found the way long enough to give me time to recall a singular air of reluctance or compulsion with which he had pointed out the path.

When I came down low enough upon the zigzag descent to see him again, I saw that he was standing between the rails on the way by which the train had lately passed, in an attitude as if he were waiting for me to appear. He had his left hand at his chin, and that left elbow rested on his right hand crossed over his breast. His attitude was one of such expectation and watchfulness that I stopped a moment, wondering at it.

I resumed my downward way and, stepping out upon the level of the railroad and drawing nearer to him, saw that he was a dark sallow man, with a dark beard and rather heavy eyebrows. His post was in as solitary and dismal a place as ever I saw. On either side, a dripping-wet wall of jagged stone, excluding all view but a strip of sky – the perspective one way, only a crooked prolongation of this great dungeon; the shorter perspective in the other direction, terminating in a gloomy red light, and the gloomier entrance to a black tunnel, in whose massive architecture there was a barbarous, depressing and forbidding air. So little sunlight ever found its way to this spot that it had an earthy deadly smell; and so much cold wind rushed through it that it struck chill to me, as if I had left the natural world.

Before he stirred, I was near enough to him to have touched him. Not even then removing his eyes from mine, he stepped back one step and lifted his hand.

This was a lonesome post to occupy (I said), and it had riveted my attention when I looked down from up yonder. A visitor was a rarity, I should suppose – not an unwelcome rarity, I hoped. In me, he merely saw a man who had been shut up within narrow limits all his life and who, being at last set free, had a newly awakened interest in these great works. To such purpose I spoke to him; but I am far from sure of the terms I used, for, besides that I am not happy in opening any conversation, there was something in the man that daunted me.

He directed a most curious look towards the red light near the tunnel's mouth, and looked all about it, as if something were missing from it, and then looked at me.

That light was part of his charge, was it not?

He answered in a low voice: "Don't you know it is?"

The monstrous thought came into my mind, as I perused the fixed eyes and the saturnine face, that this was a spirit, not a man. I have speculated since, whether there may have been infection in his mind.

In my turn, I stepped back. But in making the action, I detected in his eyes some latent fear of me. This put the monstrous thought to flight.

"You look at me," I said, forcing a smile, "as if you had a dread of me."

"I was doubtful," he returned, "whether I had seen you before."

"Where?"

He pointed to the red light he had looked at.

"There?" I said.

Intently watchful of me, he replied (but without sound), "Yes."

"My good fellow, what should I do there? However, be that as it may, I never was there, you may swear."

"I think I may," he rejoined. "Yes. I am sure I may."

His manner cleared, like my own. He replied to my remarks with readiness, and in well-chosen words. Had he much to do there? Yes – that was to say, he had enough responsibility to bear; but exactness and watchfulness were what was required of him, and of actual work – manual labour – he had next to none. To change that signal, to trim those lights and to turn this iron handle now and then was all he had to do under that head. Regarding those many long and lonely hours of which I seemed to make so much, he could only say that the routine of his life had shaped itself into that form, and he had grown used to it. He had taught himself a language down here – if only to know it by sight and to have formed his own crude ideas of its pronunciation could be called learning it. He had also worked at fractions and decimals, and tried a little algebra; but he was, and had been as a boy, a poor hand at figures. Was it necessary for him when on duty always to remain in that channel of damp air, and could he never rise into the sunshine from between those high stone walls? Why, that depended upon times and circumstances. Under some conditions there would be less upon the line than under others, and the same held good as to certain hours of the day and night. In bright weather, he did choose occasions for getting a little above these lower shadows; but, being at all times liable to be called by his electric bell, and at such times listening for it with redoubled anxiety, the relief was less than I would suppose.

He took me into his box, where there was a fire, a desk for an official book in which he had to make certain entries, a telegraphic instrument with its dial face and needles, and the little bell of which he had spoken. On my trusting that he would excuse the remark that he had been well educated, and (I hoped I might say without offence) perhaps educated above that station, he observed that instances of slight incongruity in such wise would rarely be found wanting among large bodies of men; that he had heard it was so in workhouses, in the police force, even in that last desperate resource, the army; and that he knew it was so, more or less, in any great railway staff. He had been, when young (if I could believe it, sitting in that hut – he scarcely could), a student of natural philosophy, and had attended lectures; but he had run wild, misused his opportunities, gone down and never risen again. He had no complaint to offer about that. He had made his bed and he lay upon it. It was far too late to make another.

All that I have here condensed he said in a quiet manner, with his grave dark regards divided between me and the fire. He threw in the word "sir" from time to time, and especially when he referred to his youth, as though to request me to understand that he claimed to be nothing but what I found him. He was several times interrupted by the little bell, and had to read off messages and send replies. Once, he had to stand without the door and display a flag as a train passed, and make some verbal communication to the driver. In the discharge of his duties I observed him to be remarkably exact and vigilant, breaking off his discourse at a syllable, and remaining silent until what he had to do was done.

In a word, I should have set this man down as one of the safest of men to be employed in that capacity, but for the circumstance that while he was speaking to me he twice broke off with a fallen colour, turned his face towards the little bell when it did NOT ring, opened the door of the hut (which was kept shut to exclude the unhealthy damp) and looked out towards the red light near the mouth of the tunnel. On both of those occasions, he came back to the fire with the inexplicable air upon him which I had remarked, without being able to define, when we were so far asunder.

Said I when I rose to leave him: "You almost make me think that I have met with a contented man."

(I am afraid I must acknowledge that I said it to lead him on.)

"I believe I used to be so," he rejoined, in the low voice in which he had first spoken; "but I am troubled, sir, I am troubled."

He would have recalled the words if he could. He had said them, however, and I took them up quickly.

"With what? What is your trouble?"

"It is very difficult to impart, sir. It is very, very difficult to speak of. If ever you make me another visit, I will try to tell you."

"But I expressly intend to make you another visit. Say, when shall it be?"

"I go off early in the morning, and I shall be on again at ten tomorrow night, sir."

"I will come at eleven."

He thanked me, and went out at the door with me. "I'll show my white light, sir," he said, in his peculiar low voice, "till you have found the way up. When you have found it, don't call out! And when you are at the top, don't call out!"

His manner seemed to make the place strike colder to me, but I said no more than, "Very well."

"And when you come down tomorrow night, don't call out! Let me ask you a parting question. What made you cry 'Halloa! Below there!' tonight?"

"Heaven knows," said I. "I cried something to that effect..."

"Not to that effect, sir. Those were the very words. I know them well."

"Admit those were the very words. I said them, no doubt, because I saw you below."

"For no other reason?"

"What other reason could I possibly have!"

"You had no feeling that they were conveyed to you in any supernatural way?"

"No."

He wished me goodnight, and held up his light. I walked by the side of the down line of rails (with a very disagreeable sensation of a train coming behind me), until I found the path. It was easier to mount than to descend, and I got back to my inn without any adventure.

Punctual to my appointment, I placed my foot on the first notch of the zigzag next night, as the distant clocks were striking eleven. He was waiting for me at the bottom, with his white light on.

"I have not called out," I said, when we came close together. "May I speak now?"

"By all means, sir."

"Goodnight then, and here's my hand."

"Goodnight, sir, and here's mine."

With that, we walked side by side to his box, entered it, closed the door and sat down by the fire.

"I have made up my mind, sir," he began, bending forward as soon as we were seated, and speaking in a tone but a little above a whisper, "that you shall not have to ask me twice what troubles me. I took you for someone else yesterday evening. That troubles me."

"That mistake?"

"No. That someone else."

"Who is it?"

"I don't know."

"Like me?"

"I don't know. I never saw the face. The left arm is across the face, and the right arm is waved. Violently waved. This way."

I followed his action with my eyes, and it was the action of an arm gesticulating with the utmost passion and vehemence: "For God's sake clear the way!"

"One moonlight night," said the man, "I was sitting here, when I heard a voice cry, 'Halloa! Below there!' I started up, looked from that door, and saw this someone else standing by the red light near the tunnel, waving as I just now showed you. The voice seemed hoarse with shouting, and it cried, 'Look out! Look out!' And then again 'Halloa! Below there! Look out!' I caught up my lamp, turned it on red and ran towards the figure, calling, 'What's wrong? What has happened? Where?' It stood just outside the blackness of the tunnel. I advanced so close upon it that I wondered at its keeping the sleeve across its eyes. I ran right up at it, and had my hand stretched out to pull the sleeve away, when it was gone."

"Into the tunnel," said I.

"No. I ran on into the tunnel, five hundred yards. I stopped and held my lamp above my head, and saw the figures of the measured distance, and saw the wet stains stealing down the walls and trickling through the arch. I ran out again, faster than I had run in (for I had a mortal abhorrence of the place upon me), and I looked all round the red light with my own red light, and I went up the iron ladder to the gallery atop of it, and I came down again, and ran back here. I telegraphed both ways, 'An alarm has been given. Is anything wrong?' The answer came back, both ways: 'All well'."

Resisting the slow touch of a frozen finger tracing out my spine, I showed him how that this figure must be a deception of his sense of sight, and how that figures, originating in disease of the delicate nerves that minister to the functions of the eye, were known to have often troubled patients, some of whom had become conscious of the nature of their affliction, and had even proved it by experiments upon themselves. "As to an imaginary cry," said I, "do but listen for a moment to the wind in this unnatural valley while we speak so low, and to the wild harp it makes of the telegraph wires!"

That was all very well, he returned, after we had sat listening for a while, and he ought to know something of the wind and the wires, he who so often passed long winter nights there, alone and watching. But he would beg to remark that he had not finished.

I asked his pardon, and he slowly added these words, touching my arm: "Within six hours after the appearance, the memorable accident on this line happened, and within ten hours the dead and wounded were brought along through the tunnel over the spot where the figure had stood."

A disagreeable shudder crept over me, but I did my best against it. It was not to be denied, I rejoined, that this was a remarkable coincidence, calculated deeply to impress his mind. But it was unquestionable that remarkable coincidences did continually occur, and they must be taken into account in dealing with such a subject. Though to be sure I must admit, I added (for I thought I saw that he was going to bring the objection to bear upon me), men of common sense did not allow much for coincidences in making the ordinary calculations of life.

He again begged to remark that he had not finished.

I again begged his pardon for being betrayed into interruptions.

"This," he said, again laying his hand upon my arm, and glancing over his shoulder with hollow eyes, "was just a year ago. Six or seven months passed, and I had recovered from the surprise and shock, when one morning, as the day was breaking, I, standing at that door, looked towards the red light, and saw the spectre again." He stopped, with a fixed look at me.

"Did it cry out?"

"No. It was silent."

"Did it wave its arm?"

"No. It leant against the shaft of the light, with both hands before the face. Like this."

Once more, I followed his action with my eyes. It was an action of mourning. I have seen such an attitude in stone figures on tombs.

"Did you go up to it?"

"I came in and sat down, partly to collect my thoughts, partly because it had turned me faint. When I went to the door again, daylight was above me, and the ghost was gone."

"But nothing followed? Nothing came of this?"

He touched me on the arm with his forefinger twice or thrice, giving a ghastly nod each time:

"That very day, as a train came out of the tunnel, I noticed, at a carriage window on my side, what looked like a confusion of hands and heads, and something waved. I saw it, just in time to signal the driver, 'Stop!' He shut off, and put his brake on, but the train drifted past here a hundred and fifty yards or more. I ran after it and, as I went along, heard terrible screams and cries. A beautiful young lady had died instantaneously in one of the compartments and was brought in here, and laid down on this floor between us."

Involuntarily, I pushed my chair back as I looked from the boards at which he pointed to himself.

"True, sir. True. Precisely as it happened, so I tell it you."

I could think of nothing to say, to any purpose, and my mouth was very dry. The wind and the wires took up the story with a long lamenting wail.

He resumed. "Now, sir, mark this, and judge how my mind is troubled. The spectre came back, a week ago. Ever since, it has been there, now and again, by fits and starts."

"At the light?"

"At the danger light."

"What does it seem to do?"

He repeated, if possible with increased passion and vehemence, that former gesticulation of "For God's sake clear the way!"

Then, he went on. "I have no peace or rest for it. It calls to me, for many minutes together, in an agonized manner, 'Below there! Look out! Look out!' It stands waving to me. It rings my little bell…"

I caught at that. "Did it ring your bell yesterday evening when I was here, and you went to the door?"

"Twice."

"Why, see," said I, "how your imagination misleads you. My eyes were on the bell, and my ears were open to the bell, and if I am a living man, it did NOT ring at those times. No, nor at any other time, except when it was rung in the natural course of physical things by the station communicating with you."

He shook his head. "I have never made a mistake as to that, yet, sir. I have never confused the spectre's ring with the man's. The ghost's ring is a strange vibration in the bell that it derives from nothing else, and I have not asserted that the bell stirs to the eye. I don't wonder that you failed to hear it. But *I* heard it."

"And did the spectre seem to be there, when you looked out?"

"It *was* there."

"Both times?"

He repeated firmly: "Both times."

"Will you come to the door with me and look for it now?"

He bit his underlip as though he were somewhat unwilling, but arose. I opened the door and stood on the step, while he stood in the doorway. There, was the danger light. There, was the dismal mouth of the tunnel. There, were the high wet stone walls of the cutting. There, were the stars above them.

"Do you see it?" I asked him, taking particular note of his face. His eyes were prominent and strained; but not very much more so, perhaps, than my own had been when I had directed them earnestly towards the same spot.

"No," he answered. "It is not there."

"Agreed," said I.

We went in again, shut the door and resumed our seats. I was thinking how best to improve this advantage, if it might be called one, when he took up the conversation in such a matter of course way, so assuming that there could be no serious question of fact between us, that I felt myself placed in the weakest of positions.

"By this time you will fully understand, sir," he said, "that what troubles me so dreadfully is the question: What does the spectre mean?"

I was not sure, I told him, that I did fully understand.

"What is its warning against?" he said, ruminating, with his eyes on the fire, and only by times turning them on me. "What is the danger? Where is the danger? There is danger overhanging, somewhere on the line. Some dreadful calamity will happen. It is not to be doubted this third time, after what has gone before. But surely this is a cruel haunting of *me*. What can I do?"

He pulled out his handkerchief and wiped the drops from his heated forehead.

"If I telegraph 'danger', on either side of me, or on both, I can give no reason for it," he went on, wiping the palms of his hands. "I should get into trouble, and do no good. They would think I was mad. This is the way it would work – Message: 'Danger! Take care!' Answer: 'What danger? Where?' Message: 'Don't know. But for God's sake take care!' They would displace me. What else could they do?"

His pain of mind was most pitiable to see. It was the mental torture of a conscientious man, oppressed beyond endurance by an unintelligible responsibility involving life.

"When it first stood under the danger light," he went on, putting his dark hair back from his head, and drawing his hands outwards across and across his temples in an extremity of feverish distress, "why not tell me where that accident was to happen – if it must happen? Why not tell me how it could be averted – if it could have been averted? When on its second coming it hid its face, why not tell me instead: 'She is going to die. Let them keep her at home'? If it came, on those two occasions, only to show me that its warnings were true, and so to prepare me for the third, why not warn me plainly now? And I, Lord help me! A mere poor signalman on this solitary station! Why not go to somebody with credit to be believed, and power to act!"

When I saw him in this state, I saw that for the poor man's sake, as well as for the public safety, what I had to do for the time was to compose his mind. Therefore, setting aside all question of reality or unreality between us, I represented to him that whoever thoroughly discharged his duty must do well, and that at least it was his comfort that he understood his duty, though he did not understand these confounding appearances. In this effort I succeeded far better than in the attempt to reason him out of his conviction. He became calm; the occupations incidental to his post, as the night advanced, began to make larger demands on his attention, and I left him at two in the morning. I had offered to stay through the night, but he would not hear of it.

That I more than once looked back at the red light as I ascended the pathway – that I did not like the red light, and that I should have slept but poorly if my bed had been under it – I see no reason to conceal. Nor did I like the two sequences of the accident and the dead girl. I see no reason to conceal that, either.

But, what ran most in my thoughts was the consideration how ought I to act, having become the recipient of this disclosure? I had proved the man to be intelligent, vigilant, painstaking and exact; but how long might he remain so, in his state of mind? Though in a subordinate position, still he held a most important trust, and would I (for instance) like to stake my own life on the chances of his continuing to execute it with precision?

Unable to overcome a feeling that there would be something treacherous in my communicating what he had told me to his superiors in the company, without first being plain with himself and proposing a middle course to him, I ultimately resolved to offer to accompany him (otherwise keeping his secret for the present) to the wisest medical practitioner we could hear of in those parts, and to take his opinion. A change in his time of duty would come round next night, he had apprised me, and he would be off an hour or two after sunrise, and on again soon after sunset. I had appointed to return accordingly.

Next evening was a lovely evening, and I walked out early to enjoy it. The sun was not yet quite down when I traversed the field path near the top of the deep cutting. I would extend my walk for an hour, I said to myself, half an hour on and half an hour back, and it would then be time to go to my signalman's box.

Before pursuing my stroll, I stepped to the brink, and mechanically looked down, from the point from which I had first seen him. I cannot describe the thrill that seized upon me when, close at the mouth of the tunnel, I saw the appearance of a man, with his left sleeve across his eyes, passionately waving his right arm.

The nameless horror that oppressed me passed in a moment, for in a moment I saw that this appearance of a man was a man indeed, and that there was a little group of other men standing at a short distance, to whom he seemed to be rehearsing the gesture he made. The danger light was not yet lighted. Against its shaft, a little low hut, entirely new to me, had been made of some wooden supports and tarpaulin. It looked no bigger than a bed.

With an irresistible sense that something was wrong – with a flashing self-reproachful fear that fatal mischief had come of my leaving the man there, and causing no one to be sent to overlook or correct what he did – I descended the notched path with all the speed I could make.

"What is the matter?" I asked the men.

"Signalman killed this morning, sir."

"Not the man belonging to that box?"

"Yes, sir."

"Not the man I know?"

"You will recognize him, sir, if you knew him," said the man who spoke for the others, solemnly uncovering his own head and raising an end of the tarpaulin, "for his face is quite composed."

"Oh! how did this happen, how did this happen?" I asked, turning from one to another as the hut closed in again.

"He was cut down by an engine, sir. No man in England knew his work better. But somehow he was not clear of the outer rail. It was just at broad day. He had struck the light, and had the lamp in his hand. As the engine came out of the tunnel, his back was towards her, and she cut him down. That man drove her, and was showing how it happened. Show the gentleman, Tom."

The man, who wore a rough dark dress, stepped back to his former place at the mouth of the tunnel:

"Coming round the curve in the tunnel, sir," he said, "I saw him at the end, like as if I saw him down a perspective glass. There was no time to check speed, and I knew him to be very careful. As he didn't seem to take heed of the whistle, I shut it off when we were running down upon him, and called to him as loud as I could call."

"What did you say?"

"I said, 'Below there! Look out! Look out! For God's sake clear the way!'"

I started.

"Ah! it was a dreadful time, sir. I never left off calling to him. I put this arm before my eyes, not to see, and I waved this arm to the last – but it was no use."

Without prolonging the narrative to dwell on any one of its curious circumstances more than on any other, I may, in closing it, point out the coincidence that the warning of the engine-driver included, not only the words which the unfortunate signalman had repeated to me as haunting him, but also the words which I myself – not he – had attached (and that only in my own mind) to the gesticulation he had imitated.

Note on the Texts

The texts in the present edition are based on the first printings of the works, as detailed in the relevant notes to the titles. The spelling and punctuation have been standardized, modernized and made consistent throughout.

Notes

p. 3, *The Bagman's Story*: From *The Pickwick Papers* (1836–37), Chapter 14.

p. 19, *The Story of the Goblins Who Stole a Sexton*: From *The Pickwick Papers*, Chapter 29.

p. 31, *The Story of the Bagman's Uncle*: From *The Pickwick Papers*, Chapter 49.

p. 49, *The Baron of Grogzwig*: From *Nicholas Nickleby* (1838–39), Chapter 6.

p. 50, *he had outdone Nimrod or Gillingwater*: A reference to the biblical hunter Nimrod (Genesis 10:9) and to a contemporary London barber who apparently kept bears under his shop, killing them from time to time – as advertised by a sign in his shop window which read: "Another young bear slaughtered this day" – to produce bear's grease to be used on men's hair.

p. 59, *A Confession Found in a Prison in the Time of Charles II*: From *Master Humphrey's Clock* (1840).

p. 59, *The treaty of Nijmegen*: One of a series of treaties, signed in the Dutch city of Nijmegen, which put an end to various European conflicts, in particular the Franco-Dutch War and the related Third Anglo-Dutch War.

p. 67, *To Be Read at Dusk*: From *The Keepsake* (1852).

p. 68, *Chiaia*: A neighbourhood on the seafront of Naples.

p. 73, *to the marionette*: To the puppet theatre.

p. 73, *It was an odd name*: The name Dellombra can be rendered in English as "McShadow".

p. 73, *Altro*: "Another" (Italian).

p. 79, *The Ghost in the Bride's Chamber*: From *The Lazy Tour of Two Idle Apprentices*, Chapter 4, in *Household Words* (1857). Although *The Lazy Tour* is a joint work by Charles Dickens and Wilkie Collins, a letter by Dickens dated 24th October 1857 confirms that he was the author of this particular story: "You will see 'our Lazy Tour' now going on in *Household Words*. It contains some descriptions (hem!) remarkable for their fanciful fidelity, and two grim stories – the first, of next Wednesday, by the cripple; the second of next Wednesday fortnight, that is to say in the Fourth Part, by your present correspondent – a Short Story – a bit of Diablerie."

p. 97, *The Haunted House*: Published in *All the Year Round* (1862).

p. 107, *the Admirable Crichton*: A reference to James Crichton (1560–82), the Scottish polymath and man of letters.

p. 108, *Rhadamantus*: A legendary king in Greek mythology, the son of Zeus and one of the judges of the dead.

p. 129, *To Be Taken with a Grain of Salt*: Published in *All the Year Round* (1865).

p. 129, *the Bookseller of Berlin... Sir David Brewster*: A reference to Mons. Nicolai, the bookseller of Berlin who wrote about being affected by spectral illusions, and the scientist David Brewster (1781–1868), the inventor of the kaleidoscope.

p. 141, *No. 1. Branch Line: The Signalman*: From *Mugby Junction*, published in *All the Year Round* (1866).

Extra Material

on

Charles Dickens's

Supernatural Short Stories

Charles Dickens's Life

Charles John Huffam Dickens was born in Portsmouth on 7th *First Years* February 1812 to John Dickens and Elizabeth Dickens, née Barrow. His father worked as a navy payroll clerk at the local dockyard, before transferring and moving his family to London in 1814, and then to Kent in 1817. It seems that this period possessed an idyllic atmosphere for ever afterwards in Dickens's mind. Much of his childhood was spent reading and rereading the books in his father's library, which included *Robinson Crusoe*, *The Vicar of Wakefield*, *Don Quixote*, Fielding, Smollett and the *Arabian Nights*. He was a promising, prize-winning pupil at school, and generally distinguished by his cleverness, sensitivity and enthusiasm, although unfortunately this was tempered by his frail and sickly constitution. It was at this time that he also had his first experience of what would become one of the abiding passions in his life: the theatre. Sadly, John Dickens's finances had become increasingly unhealthy, a situation which was worsened when he was transferred to London in 1822. This relocation, which entailed a termination in his schooling, distressed Charles, though he slowly came to be fascinated with the teeming, squalid streets of London.

In London, however, family finances continued to plummet *Bankruptcy and the Warehouse* until the Dickenses were facing bankruptcy. A family connection, James Lamert, offered to employ Charles at the Warren's Blacking Warehouse, which he was managing, and Dickens started working there in February 1824. He spent between six months and a year there, and the experience would prove to have a profound and lasting effect on him. The work was drudgery – sealing and labelling pots of black paste all day – and his only companions were uneducated working-class boys. His discontent at the situation was compounded by the fact that his talented older sister was sent to the Royal Academy of Music, while he was left in the warehouse.

John Dickens was finally arrested for debt and taken to Marshalsea Prison in Southwark on 20th February 1824, his wife and children (excluding Charles) moving in with him in order to save money. Meanwhile, Charles found lodgings with an intimidating old lady called Mrs Roylance (on whom he apparently modelled Mrs Pipchin in *Dombey and Son*) in Little College Street, later moving to Lant Street in Borough, which was closer to the prison. At the end of May 1824, John Dickens was released, and gradually paid off creditors as he attempted to start a new life for himself and his family. However, for some time afterwards Charles reluctantly pursued his employment at the blacking factory, as it seems his mother was unwilling to take him out of it, and even tried to arrange for him to return after he did leave. It appears that he was only removed from the warehouse after his father had quarrelled with James Lamert. The stint at the blacking factory was so profoundly humiliating for Dickens that throughout his life he apparently never mentioned this experience to any of those close to him, revealing it only in a fragment of a memoir written in 1848 and presented to his biographer John Forster: "No words can express the secret agony of my soul as I sunk into this companionship, compared these everyday associates with those of my happier childhood, and felt my early hopes of growing up to be a learned and distinguished man crushed in my breast."

School and Work in London   Fortunately he was granted some respite from hard labour when he was sent to be educated at the Wellington House Academy on Hampstead Road. Although the standard of teaching he received was apparently mediocre, the two years he spent at the school were idyllic compared to his warehouse experience, and Charles took advantage of them by making friends his own age and participating in school drama. Regrettably he had to leave the Academy in 1827, when the family finances were in turmoil once again. He found employment as a junior clerk in a solicitor's office, a job that, although routine and somewhat unfulfilling, enabled Dickens to become familiar with the ways of the London courts and the jargon of the legal profession – which he would later frequently lampoon in his novels. On reaching his eighteenth birthday, Dickens enrolled as a reader at the British Museum, determined to make up for the inadequacies of his education by studying the books in its collection, and taught himself shorthand in the hope of taking on journalistic work.

In less than a year he set himself up as a freelance law reporter, initially covering the civil law courts known as Doctors' Commons – which he did with some brio, though he found it slightly tedious – and in 1831 advanced to the press gallery of the House of Commons. His reputation as a reporter was growing steadily, and in 1834 he joined the staff of the *Morning Chronicle*, one of the leading daily newspapers. During this period, he observed and commented on some of the most socially significant debates of the time, such as the Reform Act of 1832, the Factory Act of 1833 and the Poor Law Amendment Act of 1834.

In 1829, he fell in love with the flirtatious and beautiful Maria Beadnell, the daughter of a wealthy banker, and he seems to have remained fixated on her for several years, although she rebuffed his advances. This disappointment spurred him on to achieve a higher station in life, and – after briefly entertaining the notion of becoming an actor – he threw himself into his work and wrote short stories in his spare time, which he had published in magazines, although without pay.   *First Love*

Soon enough his work for the *Morning Chronicle* was not limited to covering parliamentary matters: in recognition of his capacity for descriptive writing, he was encouraged to write reviews and sketches, and cover important meetings, dinners and election campaigns – which he reported on with enthusiasm. Written under the pseudonym "Boz", his sketches on London street life – published in the *Morning Chronicle* and then also in its sister paper, the *Evening Chronicle* – were highly rated and gained a popular following. Things were also looking up in Dickens's personal life, as he fell in love with Catherine Hogarth, the daughter of the editor of the *Evening Chronicle*: they became engaged in May 1835, and married on 2nd April 1836 at St Luke's Church in Chelsea, honeymooning in Kent afterwards. At this time his literary career began to gain momentum: first his writings on London were compiled under the title *Sketches by Boz* and printed in an illustrated two-volume edition, and then, just a few days before his wedding, *The Pickwick Papers* began to be published in monthly instalments – becoming the best-selling serialization since Lord Byron's *Childe Harold's Pilgrimage*.   *Marriage and First Major Publication*

At the end of 1836, Dickens resigned from the *Morning Chronicle* to concentrate on his literary endeavours, and met John Forster, who was to remain a lifelong friend. He helped Dickens to manage the business and legal side of his life, as well as acting as a trusted literary adviser and biographer. Forster's acumen for resolving complex situations was particularly welcome at this point, since, following the resounding success of *The Pickwick Papers*, Dickens had over-committed himself to a number of projects, with newspapers and publishers eager to capitalize on the latest literary sensation, and the deals and payments agreed no longer reflected his stature as an author.   *Success*

In January 1837, Catherine gave birth to the couple's first child, also called Charles, which prompted the young Dickens family to move from their lodgings in Furnival's Inn in Holborn to a house on 48 Doughty Street. The following month *Oliver Twist* started appearing in serial form in *Bentley's Miscellany*, which lifted the author's name to new heights. This period of domestic bliss and professional fulfilment was tragically interrupted when Catherine's sister Mary suddenly died in May at the age of seventeen. Dickens was devastated and had to interrupt work on *The Pickwick Papers* and *Oliver Twist*; this event would have a deep impact on his world view and his art. But his literary productivity would soon continue unabated; hot on the tail of *Oliver Twist* came *Nicholas Nickleby* (1838–39) and *The Old Curiosity Shop* (1840–41). By this stage, he was the leading author of the day, frequenting high society and meeting luminaries such as his idol, Thomas Carlyle. Consequently he moved to a grand Georgian house near Regent's Park, and frequently holidayed in a house in Broadstairs in Kent.

Whereas his previous novels had all more or less followed his successful formula of comedy, melodrama and social satire, Dickens opted for a different approach for his next major work, *Barnaby Rudge*, a purely historical novel. He found the writing of this book particularly arduous, so he decided that after five years of intensive labour he needed a sabbatical, and persuaded his publishers Chapman and Hall to grant him a year's leave with a monthly advance of £150 on his future earnings. During this year he would visit America and keep a notebook on his travels, with a view to getting it published on his return.

First Visit to America Dickens journeyed by steamship to Halifax, Nova Scotia, accompanied by his wife, in January 1842, and the couple would spend almost five months travelling around North America, visiting cities such as Boston, New York, Philadelphia, Cincinnati, Louisville, Toronto and Montreal. He was greeted by crowds of enthusiastic well-wishers wherever he went, and met countless important figures such as Henry Wadsworth Longfellow, Edgar Allan Poe and President John Tyler, but after the initial exhilaration of this fanfare he found it exhausting and overwhelming. The trip also brought about its share of disillusionment: having cherished romantic dreams of America being free from the corruption and snobbery of Europe, he was increasingly appalled by certain aspects of the New World, such as slavery, the treatment of prisoners and, perhaps most of all, the refusal of America to sign an international copyright agreement to prevent his works being pirated in America.

He wrote articles and made speeches condemning these practices, which resulted in a considerable amount of press hostility.

Having returned to England in the summer of 1842, he published *Back Home* his record of the trip under the title of *American Notes* and the first instalment of *Martin Chuzzlewit* later that year. Unfortunately neither of the two were quite as successful as he or his publishers would have hoped, although Dickens believed *Martin Chuzzlewit* (1842–44) was his finest work to date. During this period, Dickens started taking a greater interest in political and social issues, particularly in the treatment of children employed in mines and factories, and in the "ragged school" movement, which provided free education for destitute children. He became acquainted with the millionaire philanthropist Angela Burdett-Coutts, and persuaded her to give financial support to a school in London. In 1843, he decided to write a seasonal tale which would highlight the plight of the poor, publishing *A Christmas Carol* to great popular success in December 1843. The following year Dickens decided to leave Chapman and Hall, as his relations with them had become increasingly strained, and persuaded his printer Bradbury and Evans to become his new publisher.

In July 1844 Dickens relocated his entire family to Genoa in order *Move to Genoa* to escape London and find new sources of inspiration – and also because life in Italy was considerably cheaper. Dickens, although at first taken aback by the decay of the Ligurian capital, appears to have been fascinated by this new country and a quick learner of its language and customs. He did not write much there, apart from another Christmas book, *The Chimes*, the publication of which occasioned a brief return to London. In all the Dickenses remained in Italy for a year, travelling around the country for three months in early 1845, before returning to England in July of that year.

In Italy, he discovered that he was apparently able mesmerically to alleviate the condition of Augusta de la Rue, the wife of a Swiss banker, who suffered from anxiety and nervous spasms. This treatment required him to spend a lot of time alone with her, and unsurprisingly Catherine was not best pleased by this turn of events. She was also worn out by the burden of motherhood: they were becoming a large family, and would eventually have a total of ten children. Catherine's sister Georgina therefore began to help out with the children. Georgina was in many ways similar to Mary, whose death had so devastated Dickens, and she became involved with Dickens's various projects.

Back in London, Dickens took part in amateur theatrical productions, and took on the task of editing the *Daily News*, a new national newspaper owned by Bradbury and Evans. However, he had severely underestimated the work involved in editing the publication and resigned after seventeen issues, though he did continue to write contributions, including a series of 'Travelling Letters' – later collected in *Pictures from Italy* (1846).

More Travels Perhaps to escape the aftermath of his resignation from the *Daily*
Abroad *News* and to focus on composing his next novel, Dickens moved his family to Lausanne in Switzerland. He enjoyed the clean, quiet and beautiful surroundings, as well as the company of the town's fellow English expatriates. He also managed to write fiction: another Christmas tale entitled *The Battle of Life* and, more significantly, the beginning of *Dombey and Son*, which began serialization in September 1846 and was an immediate success.

It was also at this point that his publisher launched a series of cheap editions of his works, in the hope of tapping into new markets. Dickens returned to London, and resumed his normal routine of socializing, amateur theatricals, letter-writing and public speaking, and also became deeply involved in charitable work, such as setting up and administering a shelter for homeless women, which was funded by Miss Burdett-Coutts. *The Haunted Man*, another Christmas story, appeared in 1848, and was followed by his next major novel, *David Copperfield* (1849–50), which received rapturous critical acclaim.

Household *Household Words* was set up at this time, a popular magazine
Words founded and edited by Dickens himself. The magazine contained fictional work by not only Dickens, but also contributors such as Gaskell and Wilkie Collins, and articles on social issues. Dickens continued with his amateur theatricals, which proved a welcome distraction, since Catherine was quite seriously ill, as was his father, who died shortly afterwards. This was followed by the sudden death of his eight-month-old daughter Dora.

The Dickenses moved house again in November 1851, this time to Tavistock House in Tavistock Square. Since it was in a dilapidated state, renovation was necessary, and Dickens personally supervised every detail of this, from the installation of new plumbing to the choice of wallpaper. *Bleak House* (1852–53), his next publication, sold well, though straight after finishing it, Dickens was in desperate need of a break. He went on holiday in France with his family, and then toured Italy with Wilkie Collins and the painter Augustus Egg. After his return to London, Dickens gave a series of public readings to larger audiences than he had been accustomed to. Dickens's histrionic talents thrived in this context and the readings were a triumph, encouraging the author to repeat the exercise throughout his career – indeed, this became a lucrative venture, with Dickens employing his friend Arthur Smith as his booking agent.

During this period Dickens's stance on current politics and society became increasingly critical, which manifested itself in the numerous satirical essays he penned and the darker, more trenchant outlook of *Bleak House* and the two novels that followed, *Hard Times* (1854) and *Little Dorrit* (1855–57). In March 1856, Dickens bought Gad's Hill Place, near Rochester, for use as a country home. He had admired it during childhood country walks with his father, who had told him he might eventually own it if he were very hard-working and persevering.

However, this acquisition of a permanent home was not accompanied by domestic felicity, as by this point Dickens's marriage was in crisis. Relations between Dickens and his wife had been worsening for some time, but it all came to a head when he became acquainted with a young actress by the name of Ellen Ternan and apparently fell in love with her. The affair may never have been consummated, but Dickens involved himself with Ellen and her family's life to an extent which alarmed Catherine, just as she had been alarmed by the excessive attentions he had paid to Mme de la Rue in Genoa. Soon enough, Dickens moved into a separate bedroom in their house, and in May 1858, Dickens and his wife formally separated. This gave rise to a flurry of speculation, including rumours that Dickens was involved in a relationship with the young actress, or even worse, his sister-in-law, Georgina Hogarth, who had opted to continue living with Dickens instead of with her sister. It seemed that some of these allegations may have originated from the Hogarths, his wife's immediate family, and Dickens reacted to this by forcing them to sign a retraction, and by issuing a public statement – against his friends' advice – in *The Times* and *Household Words*. Furthermore, in August of that year one of Dickens's private letters was leaked to the press, which placed the blame for the breakdown of their marriage entirely on Catherine's shoulders, accused her of being a bad mother and insinuated that she was mentally unstable. After some initial protests, Catherine made no further effort to defend herself, and lived a quiet life until her death twenty years later. She apparently never met Dickens again, but never stopped caring about him, and followed his career and publications assiduously.

This conflict in Dickens's personal affairs also had an effect on his professional life: in 1859 the author fell out with Bradbury and Evans after they had refused to run another statement about

The End of the Marriage

All the Year Round

his private life in one of their publications, the satirical magazine *Punch*. This led him to transfer back to Chapman and Hall and to found a new weekly periodical *All the Year Round*. His first contribution to the magazine was his highly successful second historical novel, *A Tale of Two Cities* (1859), an un-Dickensian work in that it was more or less devoid of comical and satirical elements. *All the Year Round* – which focused more on fiction and less on journalistic pieces than its predecessor – maintained very healthy circulation figures, especially as the second novel to be serialized was the tremendously popular *The Woman in White* by Wilkie Collins, who became a regular collaborator. Dickens also arranged with the New York publisher J.M. Emerson & Co. for his journal to appear across the Atlantic. In December 1860, Dickens began to serialize what would become one of his best-loved novels, the deeply autobiographical *Great Expectations* (1860–61).

Our Mutual Friend   Between the final instalment of *Great Expectations* and the first instalment of his next and final completed novel, *Our Mutual Friend*, there was an uncharacteristically long three-year gap. This period was marked by two deaths in the family in 1863: that of his mother – which came as a relief more than anything, as she had been declining into senility for some time, and Dickens's feeling for her were ambivalent at best – and that of his second son, Walter – for whom Dickens grieved much more deeply. He chewed over ideas for *Our Mutual Friend* for at least two years and only began seriously composing it in early 1864, with serialization beginning in May. Although the book is now widely considered a masterpiece, it met with a tepid reception at the time, as readers did not entirely understand it.

Staplehurst Train Disaster   On 9th June 1865, Dickens experienced a traumatic incident: travelling back from France with Ellen Ternan and her mother, he was involved in a serious railway accident at Staplehurst, in which ten people lost their lives. Dickens was physically unharmed, but nevertheless profoundly affected by it, having spent hours tending the dying and injured with brandy. He drew on the experience in the writing of one of his best short stories, 'The Signalman'.

Final Years   Following the success of his public readings in Britain, Dickens had been contemplating a tour of the United States, and finally embarked on a second trip to America from December 1867 to April 1868. This turned out to be a very lucrative visit, but the exhaustion occasioned by his punishing schedule proved to be disastrous for his health. He began a farewell tour around England in 1868, incorporating a spectacular piece derived from *Oliver Twist*'s scene of Nancy's murder, but was forced to abandon the tour on the instructions of his doctors after he had a stroke in April 1869. Against medical advice, he insisted on giving a series of twelve final readings in London in 1870. These were very well received, many of those who attended commenting that he had never read so well as then. While in London, he had a private audience with Queen Victoria, and met the Prime Minister.

Dickens immersed himself in writing another major novel, *The Mystery of Edwin Drood*, the first six instalments of which were a critical and financial success. Tragically this novel was never to be completed, as Dickens died on 9th June 1870, having suffered a stroke on the previous day. He had wished to be buried in a small graveyard in Rochester, but this was overridden by a nationwide demand that he should be laid to rest in Westminster Abbey. This was done on 14th June 1870, after a strictly private ceremony which he had insisted on in his will.

Death

Charles Dickens's Works

As seen in the account of his life above, Charles Dickens was an immensely prolific writer, not only of novels but of countless articles, sketches, occasional writings and travel accounts, published in newspapers, magazines and in volume form. Descriptions of his most famous works can be found below.

Sketches by Boz, a revised and expanded collection of Dickens's newspaper pieces, was published in two volumes by John Macrone on 8th February 1836. The book was composed of sketches of London life, manners and society. It was an immediate success, and was praised by critics for the "startling fidelity" of its descriptions.

Sketches by Boz

The first instalment of Dickens's first serialized novel, *The Pickwick Papers*, appeared in March 1836. Initially Dickens's contributions were subordinate to those of the illustrator Robert Seymour, but as the series continued, this relationship was inverted, with Dickens's writing at the helm. This led to an upsurge in sales, until *The Pickwick Papers* became a fully fledged literary phenomenon, with circulation rocketing to 40,000 by the final instalment in November 1837. The book centres around the Pickwick Club and its founder, Mr Pickwick, who travels around the country with his companions Mr Winkle, Mr Snodgrass and Mr Tupman, and consists of various loosely connected and light-hearted adventures, with hints of the social satire which would pervade his mature fiction. There is no overall plot, as Dickens invented one episode at a time and, reacting to popular feedback, would switch the emphasis to the most successful characters.

The Pickwick Papers

Oliver Twist

Dickens's first coherently structured novel, *Oliver Twist*, was serialized in *Bentley's Miscellany* from February 1837 to April 1839, with illustrations by the famous caricaturist George Cruikshank. Subtitled *A Parish Boy's Progress*, in reference to Hogarth's *A Rake's Progress* and *A Harlot's Progress* cycles, Dickens tells the story of a young orphan's life and ordeals in London – which had never before been the substance of a novel – as he flees the workhouse and unhappy apprenticeship of his childhood to London, where he falls in with a criminal gang led by the malicious Fagin, before eventually discovering the secret of his origins. *Oliver Twist* publicly addressed issues such as workhouses and child exploitation by criminals – and this preoccupation with social ills and the plight of the downtrodden would become a hallmark of Dickens's fiction.

Nicholas Nickleby

Dickens's next published novel – the serialization of which for a while overlapped with that of *Oliver Twist* – was *Nicholas Nickleby*, which revolves around its eponymous hero – again an impoverished young man, though an older one this time – as he tenaciously overcomes the odds to establish himself in the world. When Nicholas's father dies penniless, the family turn to their uncle Ralph Nickleby for assistance, but he turns out to be a mean-spirited miser, and only secures menial positions for Nicholas and his sister Kate. Nicholas is sent to work in Dotheboys Hall, a dreadful Yorkshire boarding school administered by the schoolmaster Wackford Squeers, while Kate endures a humiliating stint at a London millinery. The plot twists and turns until both end up finding love and a secure position in life. Dickens's satire is more trenchant, particularly with regard to Yorkshire boarding schools, which were notorious at the time. Interestingly, within ten years of *Nicholas Nickleby*'s publication all the schools in question were closed down. Overall though, the tone is jovial and the plot is rambling and entertaining, much in the vein of Dickens's eighteenth-century idols Fielding and Smollett.

The Old Curiosity Shop

The Old Curiosity Shop started out as a piece in the short-lived weekly magazine that Dickens was editing, *Master Humphrey's Clock*, which began publication in April 1840. It was intended to be a miscellany of one-off stories, but as sales were disappointing, Dickens was forced to adapt the 'Personal Adventures of Master Humphrey' into a full-length narrative that would be the most Romantic and fairy-tale-like of Dickens's novels, with some of his greatest humorous passages. The story revolves around Little Nell, a young girl who lives with her grandfather in his eponymous shop, and recounts how the two struggle to release themselves from the grip of the evil usurer dwarf Quilp. By the end of its serialization, circulation had reached the phenomenal figure of 100,000, and Little Nell's death had famously plunged thousands of readers into grief.

As seen above, Dickens took on a different genre for his next *Barnaby Rudge* major work of fiction, *Barnaby Rudge*: this was a historical novel, addressing the anti-Catholic Gordon riots of 1780, which focused on a village outside London and its protagonist, a simpleton called Barnaby Rudge. The novel was serialized in *Master Humphrey's Clock* from 1840 to 1841, and met with a lukewarm reception from the reading public, who thirsted for more novels in the vein of *The Old Curiosity Shop*.

Dickens therefore gave up on the historical genre, and began *Martin* serializing the more picaresque *Martin Chuzzlewit* from December *Chuzzlewit* 1842 to June 1844. The book explores selfishness and its consequences: the eponymous protagonist is the grandson and heir of the wealthy Martin Chuzzlewit senior, and is surrounded by relatives eager to inherit his money. But when Chuzzlewit junior finds himself disinherited and penniless, he has to make his own way in the world. Although it was a step forwards in his writing, being the first of his works to be written with a fully predetermined overall design, it sold poorly – partly due to the fact that publishing in general was experiencing a slump in the early 1840s. In a bid to revive sales, Dickens adjusted the plot during the serialization and sent the title character to America – his own recent visit there providing much material.

In 1843, Dickens had the idea of writing a small seasonal *Christmas Books* Christmas book, which would aim to revive the spirit of the *and The Haunted* holiday and address the social problems that he was increasingly *House* interested in. The resulting work, *A Christmas Carol*, was a phenomenal success at the time, and the tale and its characters, such as Scrooge, Bob Cratchit and Tiny Tim, have now achieved an iconic status. Thackeray famously praised it as "a national benefit and to every man or woman who reads it a personal kindness". Dickens published four more annual Christmas novellas – *The Chimes*, *The Cricket on the Hearth*, *The Battle of Life* and *The Haunted Man* – which were successful at the time, but did not quite live up to the classic appeal of *A Christmas Carol*. After *The Haunted Man*, Dickens discontinued his Christmas books, but he included annual Christmas stories in his magazines *Household Words* and *All the Year Round*. Each set of these stories usually took the form of a miniature *Arabian Nights*, with a number of unrelated short stories linked together through a frame narrative – typically Dickens wrote the frame narrative, and invited other writers to supply the stories included within it, writing the occasional one of them himself. *The Haunted House* appeared in *All the Year Round* in 1862.

Dombey and Son   While living in Lausanne, Dickens composed *Dombey and Son*, which was serialized between October 1846 and April 1848 by Bradbury and Evans with highly successful results. The novel centres on Paul Dombey, the wealthy owner of a shipping company, who desperately wants a son to take over his business after his death. Unfortunately his wife dies giving birth to the longed-for successor, Paul Dombey junior, a sickly child who does not survive long. Although Dombey – who neglects his fatherly responsibilities towards his daughter Florence – is for the most part unsympathetic, he ends up turning a new leaf and becoming a devoted family man. Significantly, this is the first of Dickens's novels for which his working notes survive, from which one can clearly see the great care and detail with which he planned the novel.

David   *David Copperfield* (1849–1850) is at once the most personal and
Copperfield   the most popular of Dickens's novels. He had tried, probably during 1847–48, to write his autobiography, but, according to his own later account, had found writing about certain aspects, such as his first love for Maria Beadnell, too painful. Instead he chose to transpose autobiographical events into a first-person *Bildungsroman*, *David Copperfield*, which drew on his personal experience of the blacking factory, journalism, his schooling at Wellington House and his love for Maria. Its depiction of the Micawbers owed much to Dickens's own parents. There was great critical acclaim for the novel, and it soon became widely held to be his greatest work.

Bleak House   For his next novel, *Bleak House* (1852–53), Dickens turned his satirical gaze on the English legal system. The focus of the novel is a long-running court case, Jarndyce and Jarndyce, the consequences of which reach from the filthy slums to the landed aristocracy. The scope of the novel may well be the broadest of all of his works, and Dickens also experimented with dual narrators, one in the third person and one in the first. He was well equipped to write on the subject matter due to his experiences as a law clerk and journalist, and his critique of the judiciary system was met with recognition by those involved in it, which helped set the stage for its reform in the 1870s.

Hard Times   *Hard Times* was Dickens's next novel, serialized in *Household Words* between April and August 1854, in which he satirically probed into social and economic issues to a degree not achieved in his other works. Using the infamous characters Thomas Gradgrind and Josiah Bounderby, he attacks utilitarianism, workers' conditions in factories, spurious usage of statistics and fact as opposed to imagination. The story is set in the fictitious northern industrial setting of Coketown, among the workers, school pupils and teachers. The shortest and most polemical of Dickens's major novels, it sold extremely well on publication, but has only recently been fully accepted into the canon of Dickens's most significant works.

Little Dorrit (1855–57) was also a darkly critical novel, satiriz- *Little Dorrit* ing the shortcomings of the government and society, with institutions such as debtor's prisons – in one of which, as seen above, Dickens's own father had been held – and the fantastically named Circumlocution Office bearing the brunt of Dickens's bile. The plot centres on the romance which develops between the characters of Little Dorrit, a paragon of virtue who has grown up in prison, and Arthur Clennam, a hapless middle-aged man who returns to England to make a living for himself after many years abroad. Although at the time many critics were hostile to the work, taking issue with what they saw as an overly convoluted plot and a lack of humour, sales were outstanding and the novel is now ranked as one of Dickens's finest.

A Tale of Two Cities is the second of Dickens's historical novels, *A Tale of Two* covering the period between 1775 and 1793, from the American *Cities* Revolution until the middle of the French Revolution. His primary source was Thomas Carlyle's *The French Revolution*. The story is of two men – Charles Darnay and Sydney Carton – who look very similar, though they are utterly different in character, who both love the same woman, Lucie Manette. The opening and closing sentences are among the most famous in literature: "It was the best of times, it was the worst of times." "It is a far, far better thing that I do, than I have ever done; it is a far, far better rest that I go to than I have ever known."

Due to a slump in circulation figures for *All the Year Round*, *Great* Dickens brought out his next novel, in December 1860, as a weekly *Expectations* serial in the magazine, instead of having it published in monthly instalments as initially intended. The sales promptly recovered, and the audience and critics were delighted to read the story which some regard as Dickens's greatest ever work, *Great Expectations* (1860–61). On publication, it was immediately acclaimed a masterpiece, and was hugely successful in America as well as England. Like *David Copperfield*, it was written in the first person as a *Bildungsroman*, though this time its protagonist, Pip, was explicitly working class. Graham Greene once commented: "Dickens had somehow miraculously varied his tone, but when I tried to analyse his success, I felt like a colour-blind man trying intellectually to distinguish one colour from another." George Orwell was moved to declare: "Psychologically the latter part of *Great Expectations* is about the best thing Dickens ever did."

Our Mutual Friend   Dickens started work on his next novel, *Our Mutual Friend* (1864–65), by 1861 at the latest. It had an unusually long gestation period, and a mixed reception when first published. However, in recent years it has been reappraised as one of his greatest works. It is probably his most challenging and complicated, although some critics, including G.K. Chesterton, have argued that the ending is rushed. It opens with a young man on his way to receive his inheritance, which he can apparently only attain if he marries a beautiful and mercenary girl, Bella Wilfer, whom he has never met. However, before he arrives, a body is found in the Thames, which is identified as being him. So instead the money passes on to the Boffins, the effects of which spread through to various parts of London society.

The Mystery of Edwin Drood   In April 1870, the first instalment of Dickens's last novel, *The Mystery of Edwin Drood*, appeared. It was the culmination of Dickens's lifelong fascination with murderers. It was favourably received, outselling *Our Mutual Friend*, but only six of the projected twelve instalments were published, as Dickens died in June of that year.

There has naturally been much speculation on how the book would have finished, and suggestions as to how it should end. As it stands, the novel is set in the fictional area of Cloisterham, which is a thinly veiled rendering of Rochester. The plot mainly focuses on the choirmaster and opium addict John Jasper, who is in love with Rosa Bud – his pupil and his nephew Edwin Drood's fiancée. The twins Helena and Neville Landless arrive in Cloisterham, and Neville is attracted to Rosa Bud. Neville and Edwin end up having a huge row one day, after which Neville leaves town, and Edwin vanishes. Neville is questioned about Edwin's disappearance, and John Jasper accuses him of murder.

Select Bibliography

Biographies:

Ackroyd, Peter, *Dickens* (London: Sinclair-Stevenson, 1990)

Forster, John, *The Life of Charles Dickens* (London: Cecil Palmer, 1872–74)

James, Elizabeth, *Charles Dickens* (London: British Library, 2004)

Kaplan, Fred, *Dickens: A Biography* (London: Hodder & Stoughton, 1988)

Smiley, Jane, *Charles Dickens* (London: Weidenfeld and Nicolson, 2002)

Additional Recommended Background Material:

Collins, Philip, ed., *Dickens: The Critical Heritage* (London: Routledge & Kegan Paul, 1971)

Fielding, K.J, *Charles Dickens: A Critical Introduction* 2nd ed. (London: Longmans, 1965)

Wilson, Angus, *The World of Charles Dickens* (London: Secker & Warburg, 1970)

On the Web:

dickens.stanford.edu

dickens.ucsc.edu

www.dickensmuseum.com

ALMA CLASSICS

ALMA CLASSICS aims to publish mainstream and lesser-known European classics in an innovative and striking way, while employing the highest editorial and production standards. By way of a unique approach the range offers much more, both visually and textually, than readers have come to expect from contemporary classics publishing.

~

1. James Hanley, *Boy*
2. D.H. Lawrence, *The First Women in Love*
3. Charlotte Brontë, *Jane Eyre*
4. Jane Austen, *Pride and Prejudice*
5. Emily Brontë, *Wuthering Heights*
6. Anton Chekhov, *Sakhalin Island*
7. Giuseppe Gioacchino Belli, *Sonnets*
8. Jack Kerouac, *Beat Generation*
9. Charles Dickens, *Great Expectations*
10. Jane Austen, *Emma*
11. Wilkie Collins, *The Moonstone*
12. D.H. Lawrence, *The Second Lady Chatterley's Lover*
13. Jonathan Swift, *The Benefit of Farting Explained*
14. Anonymous, *Dirty Limericks*
15. Henry Miller, *The World of Sex*
16. Jeremias Gotthelf, *The Black Spider*
17. Oscar Wilde, *The Picture Of Dorian Gray*
18. Erasmus, *Praise of Folly*
19. Henry Miller, *Quiet Days in Clichy*
20. Cecco Angiolieri, *Sonnets*
21. Fyodor Dostoevsky, *Humiliated and Insulted*
22. Jane Austen, *Sense and Sensibility*
23. Theodor Storm, *Immensee*
24. Ugo Foscolo, *Sepulchres*
25. Boileau, *Art of Poetry*
26. Georg Kaiser, *Plays Vol. 1*
27. Émile Zola, *Ladies' Delight*
28. D.H. Lawrence, *Selected Letters*
29. Alexander Pope, *The Art of Sinking in Poetry*

30. E.T.A. Hoffmann, *The King's Bride*
31. Ann Radcliffe, *The Italian*
32. Prosper Mérimée, *A Slight Misunderstanding*
33. Giacomo Leopardi, *Canti*
34. Giovanni Boccaccio, *Decameron*
35. Annette von Droste-Hülshoff, *The Jew's Beech*
36. Stendhal, *Life of Rossini*
37. Eduard Mörike, *Mozart's Journey to Prague*
38. Jane Austen, *Love and Friendship*
39. Leo Tolstoy, *Anna Karenina*
40. Ivan Bunin, *Dark Avenues*
41. Nathaniel Hawthorne, *The Scarlet Letter*
42. Sadeq Hedayat, *Three Drops of Blood*
43. Alexander Trocchi, *Young Adam*
44. Oscar Wilde, *The Decay of Lying*
45. Mikhail Bulgakov, *The Master and Margarita*
46. Sadeq Hedayat, *The Blind Owl*
47. Alain Robbe-Grillet, *Jealousy*
48. Marguerite Duras, *Moderato Cantabile*
49. Raymond Roussel, *Locus Solus*
50. Alain Robbe-Grillet, *In the Labyrinth*
51. Daniel Defoe, *Robinson Crusoe*
52. Robert Louis Stevenson, *Treasure Island*
53. Ivan Bunin, *The Village*
54. Alain Robbe-Grillet, *The Voyeur*
55. Franz Kafka, *Dearest Father*
56. Geoffrey Chaucer, *Canterbury Tales*
57. Ambrose Bierce, *The Monk and the Hangman's Daughter*
58. Fyodor Dostoevsky, *Winter Notes on Summer Impressions*
59. Bram Stoker, *Dracula*
60. Mary Shelley, *Frankenstein*
61. Johann Wolfgang von Goethe, *Elective Affinities*
62. Marguerite Duras, *The Sailor from Gibraltar*
63. Robert Graves, *Lars Porsena*
64. Napoleon Bonaparte, *Aphorisms and Thoughts*
65. Joseph von Eichendorff, *Memoirs of a Good-for-Nothing*
66. Adelbert von Chamisso, *Peter Schlemihl*
67. Pedro Antonio de Alarcón, *The Three-Cornered Hat*
68. Jane Austen, *Persuasion*
69. Dante Alighieri, *Rime*
70. Anton Chekhov, *The Woman in the Case and Other Stories*
71. Mark Twain, *The Diaries of Adam and Eve*
72. Jonathan Swift, *Gulliver's Travels*

73. Joseph Conrad, *Heart of Darkness*
74. Gottfried Keller, *A Village Romeo and Juliet*
75. Raymond Queneau, *Exercises in Style*
76. Georg Büchner, *Lenz*
77. Giovanni Boccaccio, *Life of Dante*
78. Jane Austen, *Mansfield Park*
79. E.T.A. Hoffmann, *The Devil's Elixirs*
80. Claude Simon, *The Flanders Road*
81. Raymond Queneau, *The Flight of Icarus*
82. Niccolò Machiavelli, *The Prince*
83. Mikhail Lermontov, *A Hero of our Time*
84. Henry Miller, *Black Spring*
85. Victor Hugo, *The Last Day of a Condemned Man*
86. D.H. Lawrence, *Paul Morel*
87. Mikhail Bulgakov, *The Life of Monsieur de Molière*
88. Leo Tolstoy, *Three Novellas*
89. Stendhal, *Travels in the South of France*
90. Wilkie Collins, *The Woman in White*
91. Alain Robbe-Grillet, *Erasers*
92. Iginio Ugo Tarchetti, *Fosca*
93. D.H. Lawrence, *The Fox*
94. Borys Conrad, *My Father Joseph Conrad*
95. James De Mille, *A Strange Manuscript Found in a Copper Cylinder*
96. Émile Zola, *Dead Men Tell No Tales*
97. Alexander Pushkin, *Ruslan and Lyudmila*
98. Lewis Carroll, *Alice's Adventures Under Ground*
99. James Hanley, *The Closed Harbour*
100. Thomas De Quincey, *On Murder Considered as One of the Fine Arts*
101. Jonathan Swift, *The Wonderful Wonder of Wonders*
102. Petronius, *Satyricon*
103. Louis-Ferdinand Céline, *Death on Credit*
104. Jane Austen, *Northanger Abbey*
105. W.B. Yeats, *Selected Poems*
106. Antonin Artaud, *The Theatre and Its Double*
107. Louis-Ferdinand Céline, *Journey to the End of the Night*
108. Ford Madox Ford, *The Good Soldier*
109. Leo Tolstoy, *Childhood, Boyhood, Youth*
110. Guido Cavalcanti, *Complete Poems*
111. Charles Dickens, *Hard Times*
112. Charles Baudelaire and Théophile Gautier, *Hashish, Wine, Opium*
113. Charles Dickens, *Haunted House*
114. Ivan Turgenev, *Fathers and Children*
115. Dante Alighieri, *Inferno*

116. Gustave Flaubert, *Madame Bovary*
117. Alexander Trocchi, *Man at Leisure*
118. Alexander Pushkin, *Boris Godunov and Little Tragedies*
119. Miguel de Cervantes, *Don Quixote*
120. Mark Twain, *Huckleberry Finn*
121. Charles Baudelaire, *Paris Spleen*
122. Fyodor Dostoevsky, *The Idiot*
123. René de Chateaubriand, *Atala and René*
124. Mikhail Bulgakov, *Diaboliad*
125. Goerge Eliot, *Middlemarch*
126. Edmondo De Amicis, *Constantinople*
127. Petrarch, *Secretum*
128. Johann Wolfgang von Goethe, *The Sorrows of Young Werther*
129. Alexander Pushkin, *Eugene Onegin*
130. Fyodor Dostoevsky, *Notes from Underground*
131. Luigi Pirandello, *Plays Vol. 1*
132. Jules Renard, *Histoires Naturelles*
133. Gustave Flaubert, *The Dictionary of Received Ideas*
134. Charles Dickens, *The Life of Our Lord*
135. D.H. Lawrence, *The Lost Girl*
136. Benjamin Constant, *The Red Notebook*
137. Raymond Queneau, *We Always Treat Women too Well*
138. Alexander Trocchi, *Cain's Book*
139. Raymond Roussel, *Impressions of Africa*
140. Llewelyn Powys, *A Struggle for Life*
141. Nikolai Gogol, *How the Two Ivans Quarrelled*
142. F. Scott Fitzgerald, *The Great Gatsby*
143. Jonathan Swift, *Directions to Servants*
144. Dante Alighieri, *Purgatory*
145. Mikhail Bulgakov, *A Young Doctor's Notebook*
146. Sergei Dovlatov, *The Suitcase*
147. Leo Tolstoy, *Hadji Murat*
148. Jonathan Swift, *The Battle of the Books*
149. F. Scott Fitzgerald, *Tender Is the Night*
150. Alexander Pushkin, *The Queen of Spades and Other Short Fiction*
151. Raymond Queneau, *The Sunday of Life*
152. Herman Melville, *Moby Dick*
153. Mikhail Bulgakov, *The Fatal Eggs*
154. Antonia Pozzi, *Poems*
155. Johann Wolfgang von Goethe, *Wilhelm Meister*
156. Anton Chekhov, *The Story of a Nobody*
157. Fyodor Dostoevsky, *Poor People*
158. Leo Tolstoy, *The Death of Ivan Ilyich*

159. Dante Alighieri, *Vita nuova*
160. Arthur Conan Doyle, *The Tragedy of Korosko*
161. Franz Kafka, *Letters to Friends, Family and Editors*
162. Mark Twain, *The Adventures of Tom Sawyer*
163. Erich Fried, *Love Poems*
164. Antonin Artaud, *Selected Works*
165. Charles Dickens, *Oliver Twist*
166. Sergei Dovlatov, *The Zone*
167. Louis-Ferdinand Céline, *Guignol's Band*
168. Mikhail Bulgakov, *Dog's Heart*
169. Rayner Heppenstall, *Blaze of Noon*
170. Fyodor Dostoevsky, *The Crocodile*
171. Anton Chekhov, *Death of a Civil Servant*
172. Georg Kaiser, *Plays Vol. 2*
173. Tristan Tzara, *Seven Dada Manifestos* and *Lampisteries*
174. Frank Wedekind, *The Lulu Plays and Other Sex Tragedies*
175. Frank Wedekind, *Spring Awakening*
176. Fyodor Dostoevsky, *The Gambler*
177. Prosper Mérimée, *The Etruscan Vase and Other Stories*
178. Edgar Allan Poe, *Tales of the Supernatural*
179. Virginia Woolf, *To the Lighthouse*
180. F. Scott Fitzgerald, *The Beautiful and Damned*
181. James Joyce, *Dubliners*
182. Alexander Pushkin, *The Captain's Daughter*
183. Sherwood Anderson, *Winesburg Ohio*
184. James Joyce, *Ulysses*
185. Ivan Turgenev, *Faust*
186. Virginia Woolf, *Mrs Dalloway*
187. Paul Scarron, *Roman Comique*
188. Sergei Dovlatov, *Pushkin Hills*
189. F. Scott Fitzgerald, *This Side of Paradise*
190. Alexander Pushkin, *Complete Lyrical Poems*
191. Luigi Pirandello, *Plays Vol. 2*
192. Ivan Turgenev, *Rudin*

To order any of our titles and for up-to-date information about our current and forthcoming publications, please visit our website on:

www.almaclassics.com